DATE DUE

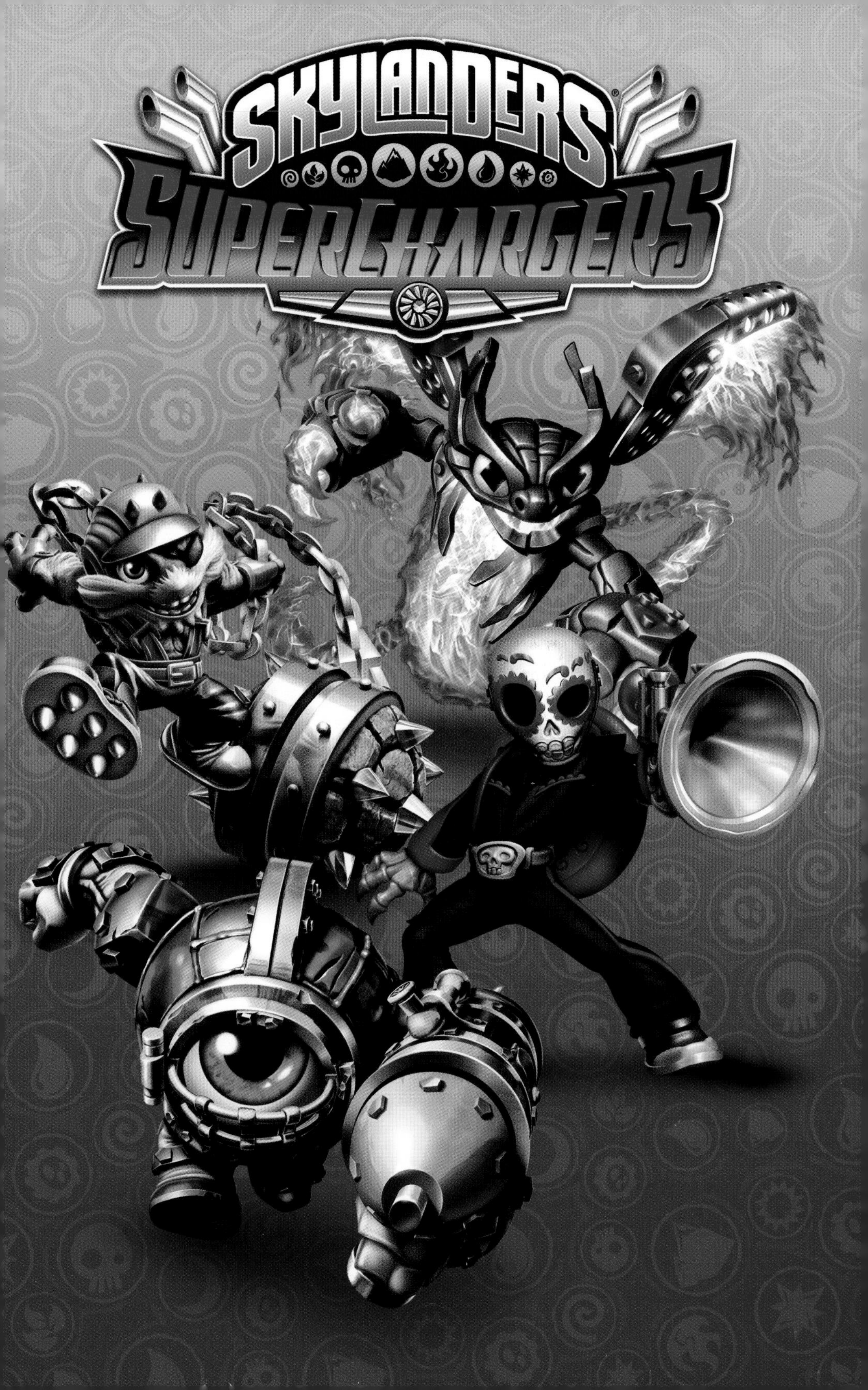
SKYLANDERS
SUPERCHARGERS

SKYLANDERS SUPERCHARGERS

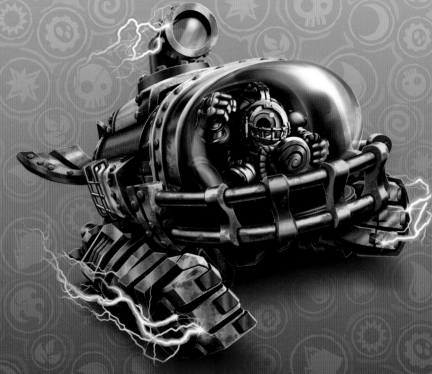

Cover Artist: **Fico Ossio**
Cover Colorist: **David Garcia Cruz**
Series Edits: **David Hedgecock**
Collection Edits: **Justin Eisinger & Alonzo Simon**
Publisher: **Ted Adams**
Collection Designer: **Tom B. Long**

For international rights, please contact **licensing@idwpublishing.com**

ISBN: 978-1-63140-581-5

19 18 17 16 1 2 3 4

IDW
www.IDWPUBLISHING.com

ACTIVISION

Ted Adams, CEO & Publisher
Greg Goldstein, President & COO
Robbie Robbins, EVP/Sr. Graphic Artist
Chris Ryall, Chief Creative Officer/Editor-in-Chief
Matthew Ruzicka, CPA, Chief Financial Officer
Dirk Wood, VP of Marketing
Lorelei Bunjes, VP of Digital Services
Jeff Webber, VP of Licensing, Digital and Subsidiary Rights
Jerry Bennington, VP of New Product Development

Facebook: **facebook.com/idwpublishing**
Twitter: **@idwpublishing**
YouTube: **youtube.com/idwpublishing**
Tumblr: **tumblr.idwpublishing.com**
Instagram:**instagram.com/idwpublishing**

Originally published as SKYLANDERS SUPERCHARGERS issues #1–3.

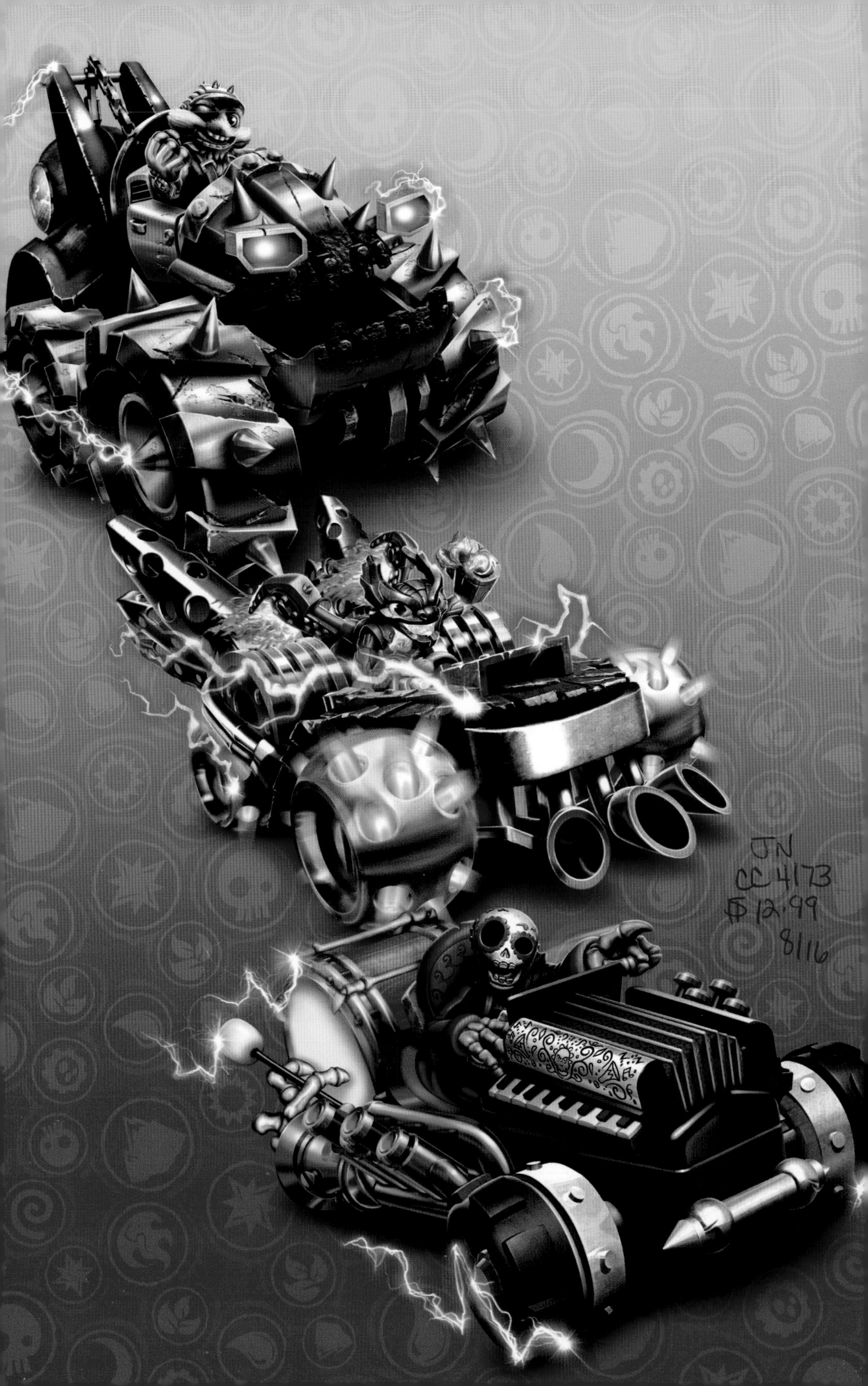

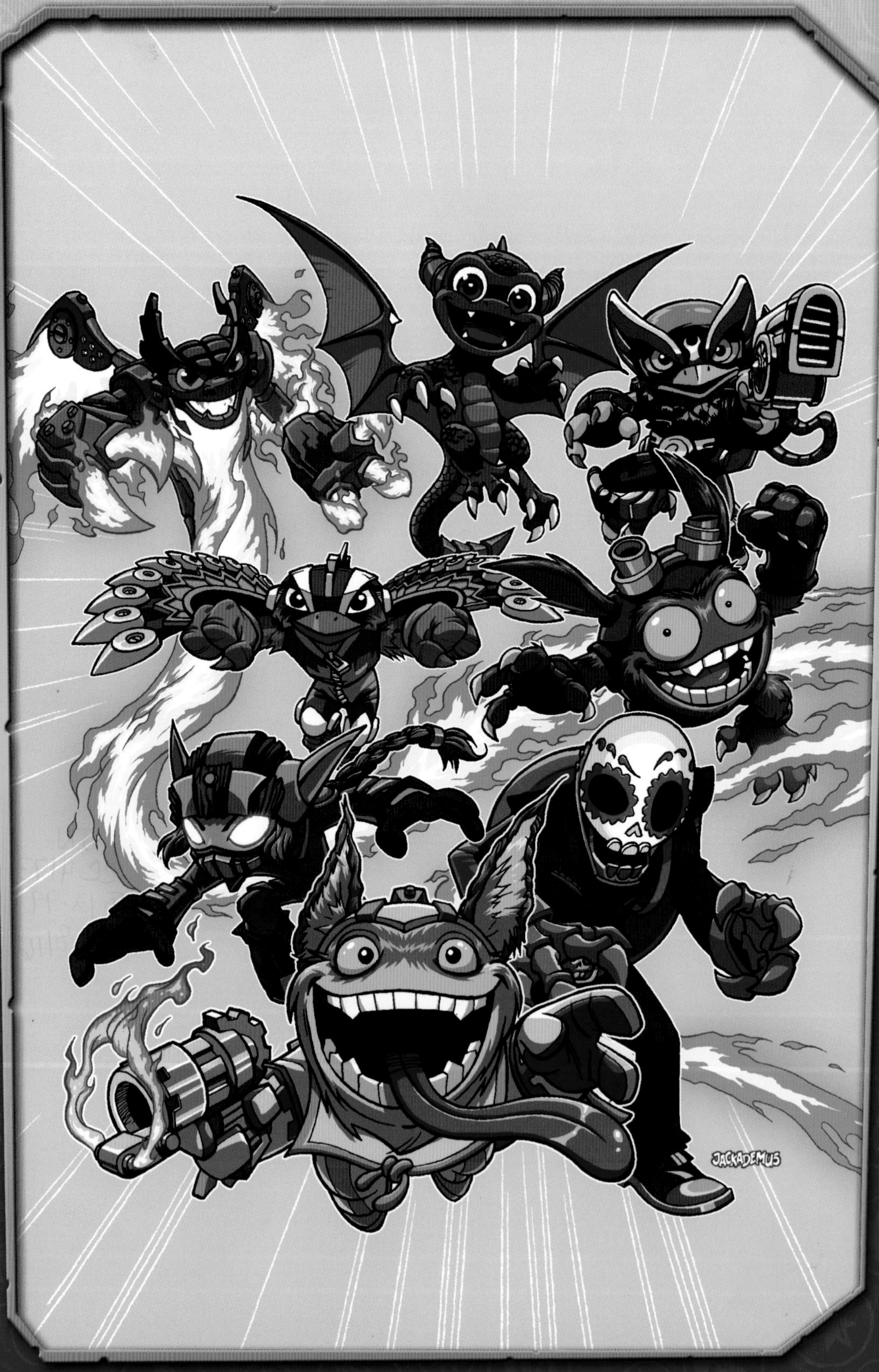
JACKADEMUS

SECRET AGENT SECRETS

Written by: **RON MARZ & DAVID A. RODRIGUEZ**
Art by: **FICO OSSIO**
Colors by: **DAVID GARCIA CRUZ**
Letters by: **DERON BENNETT**

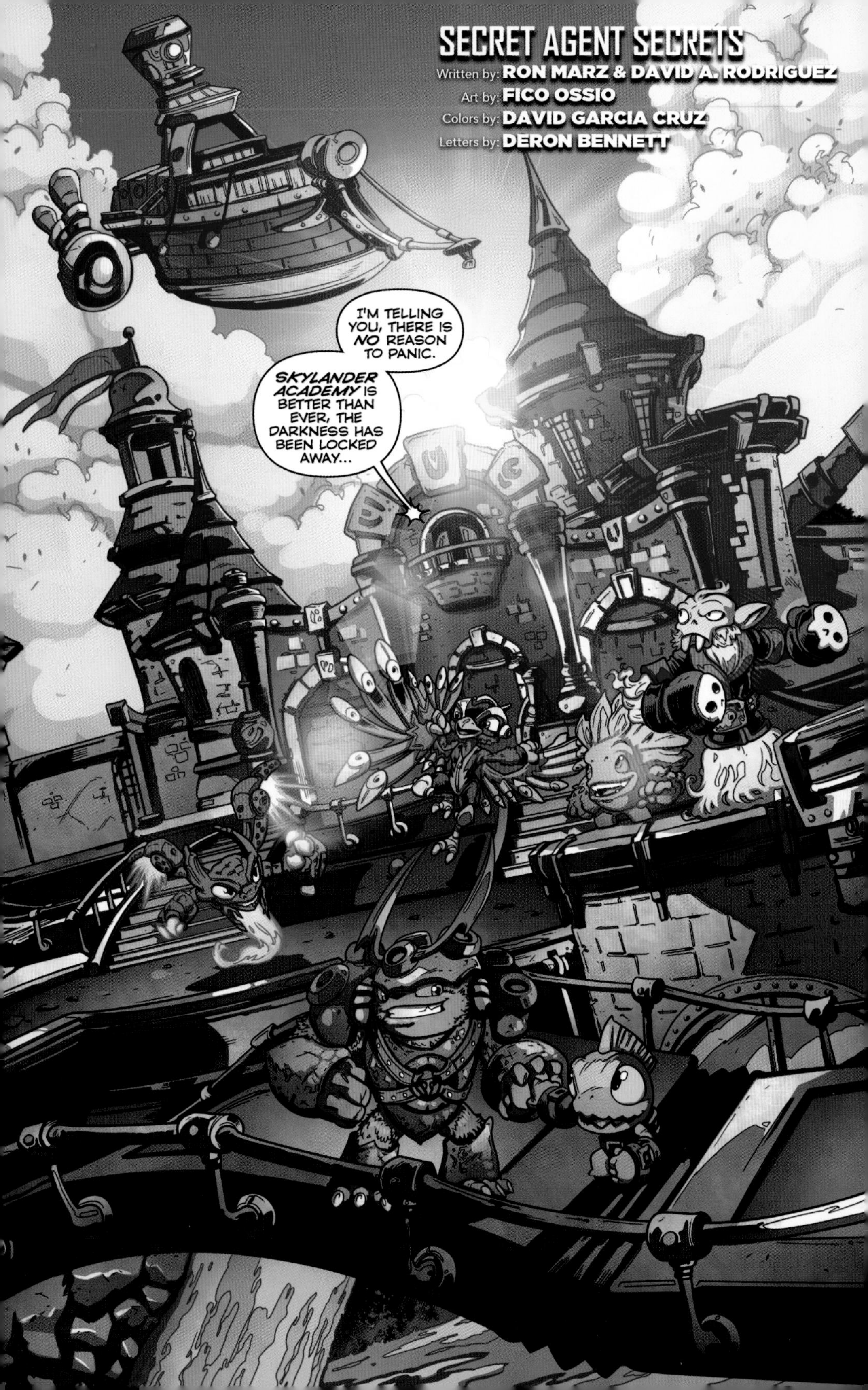

I'M TELLING YOU, THERE IS *NO* REASON TO PANIC.
SKYLANDER ACADEMY IS BETTER THAN EVER, THE DARKNESS HAS BEEN LOCKED AWAY...

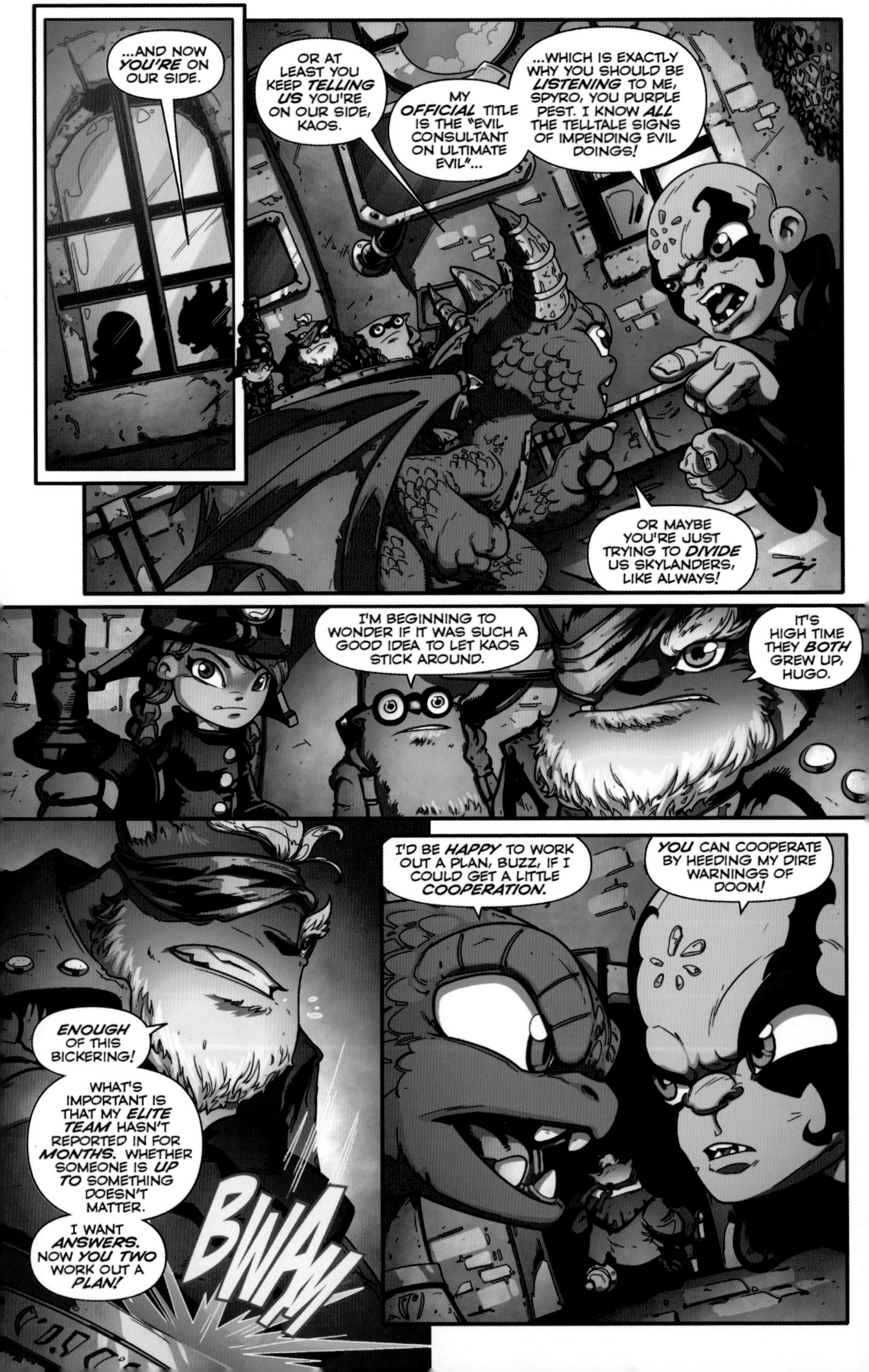
...AND NOW YOU'RE ON OUR SIDE.
OR AT LEAST YOU KEEP TELLING US YOU'RE ON OUR SIDE, KAOS.
MY OFFICIAL TITLE IS THE "EVIL CONSULTANT ON ULTIMATE EVIL"...
...WHICH IS EXACTLY WHY YOU SHOULD BE LISTENING TO ME, SPYRO, YOU PURPLE PEST. I KNOW ALL THE TELLTALE SIGNS OF IMPENDING EVIL DOINGS!
OR MAYBE YOU'RE JUST TRYING TO DIVIDE US SKYLANDERS, LIKE ALWAYS!
I'M BEGINNING TO WONDER IF IT WAS SUCH A GOOD IDEA TO LET KAOS STICK AROUND.
IT'S HIGH TIME THEY BOTH GREW UP, HUGO.
ENOUGH OF THIS BICKERING!
WHAT'S IMPORTANT IS THAT MY ELITE TEAM HASN'T REPORTED IN FOR MONTHS. WHETHER SOMEONE IS UP TO SOMETHING DOESN'T MATTER.
I WANT ANSWERS. NOW YOU TWO WORK OUT A PLAN!
BWAM
I'D BE HAPPY TO WORK OUT A PLAN, BUZZ, IF I COULD GET A LITTLE COOPERATION.
YOU CAN COOPERATE BY HEEDING MY DIRE WARNINGS OF DOOM!

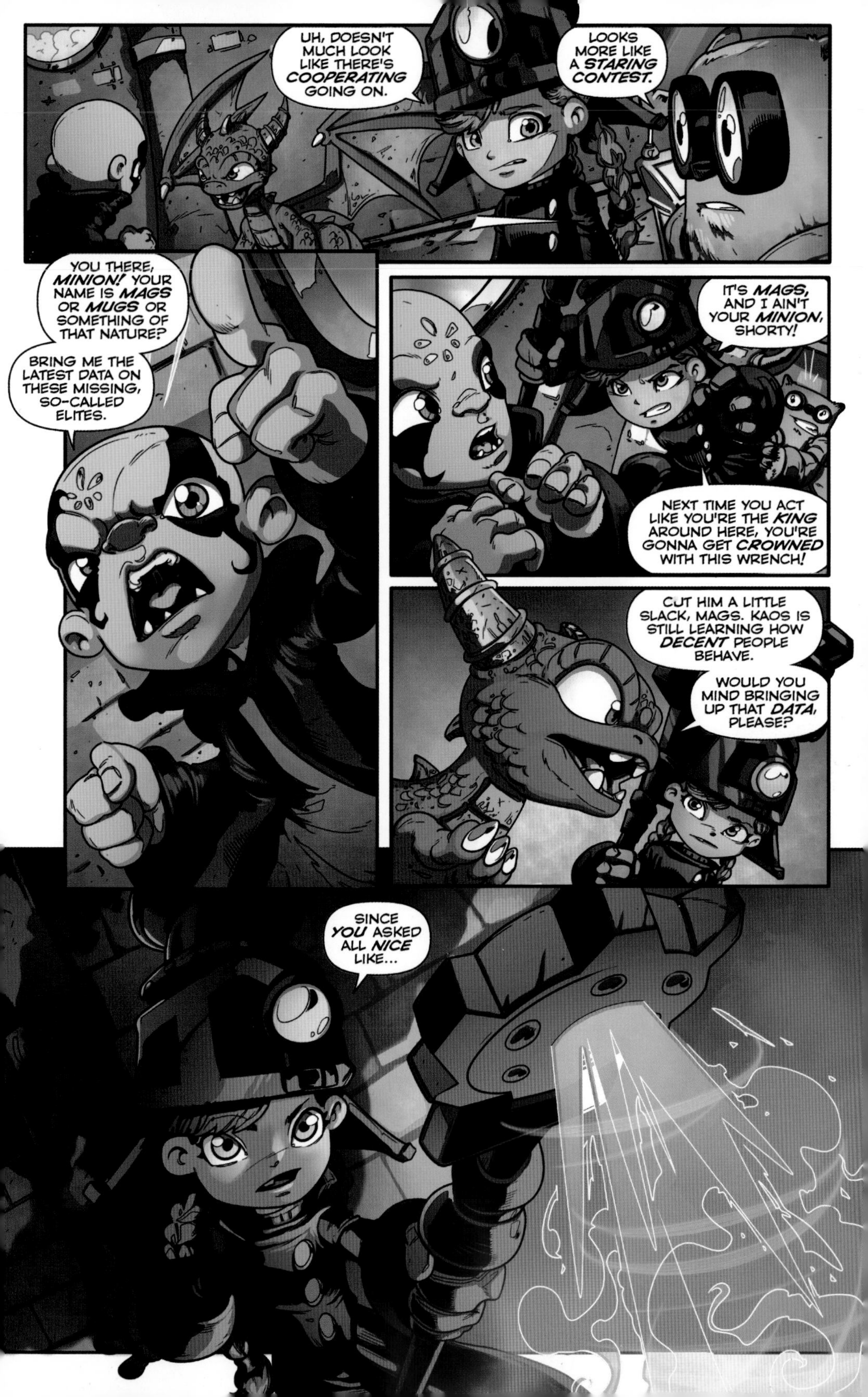
UH, DOESN'T MUCH LOOK LIKE THERE'S COOPERATING GOING ON.
LOOKS MORE LIKE A STARING CONTEST.
YOU THERE, MINION! YOUR NAME IS MAGS OR MUGS OR SOMETHING OF THAT NATURE?
BRING ME THE LATEST DATA ON THESE MISSING, SO-CALLED ELITES.
IT'S MAGS, AND I AIN'T YOUR MINION, SHORTY!
NEXT TIME YOU ACT LIKE YOU'RE THE KING AROUND HERE, YOU'RE GONNA GET CROWNED WITH THIS WRENCH!
CUT HIM A LITTLE SLACK, MAGS. KAOS IS STILL LEARNING HOW DECENT PEOPLE BEHAVE.
WOULD YOU MIND BRINGING UP THAT DATA, PLEASE?
SINCE YOU ASKED ALL NICE LIKE...

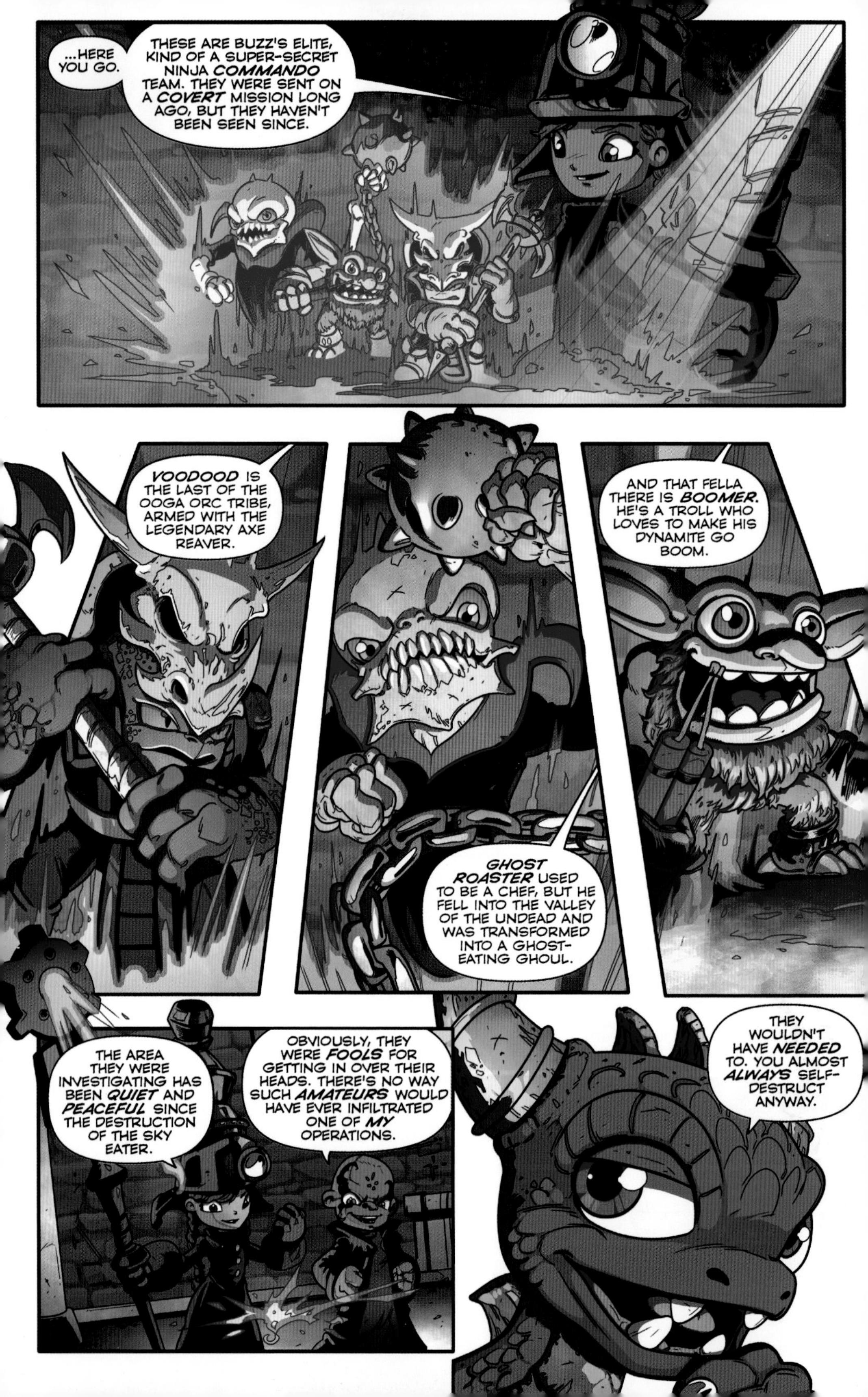
...HERE YOU GO.
THESE ARE BUZZ'S ELITE, KIND OF A SUPER-SECRET NINJA COMMANDO TEAM. THEY WERE SENT ON A COVERT MISSION LONG AGO, BUT THEY HAVEN'T BEEN SEEN SINCE.
VOODOOD IS THE LAST OF THE OOGA ORC TRIBE, ARMED WITH THE LEGENDARY AXE REAVER.
GHOST ROASTER USED TO BE A CHEF, BUT HE FELL INTO THE VALLEY OF THE UNDEAD AND WAS TRANSFORMED INTO A GHOST-EATING GHOUL.
AND THAT FELLA THERE IS BOOMER. HE'S A TROLL WHO LOVES TO MAKE HIS DYNAMITE GO BOOM.
THE AREA THEY WERE INVESTIGATING HAS BEEN QUIET AND PEACEFUL SINCE THE DESTRUCTION OF THE SKY EATER.
OBVIOUSLY, THEY WERE FOOLS FOR GETTING IN OVER THEIR HEADS. THERE'S NO WAY SUCH AMATEURS WOULD HAVE EVER INFILTRATED ONE OF MY OPERATIONS.
THEY WOULDN'T HAVE NEEDED TO. YOU ALMOST ALWAYS SELF-DESTRUCT ANYWAY.

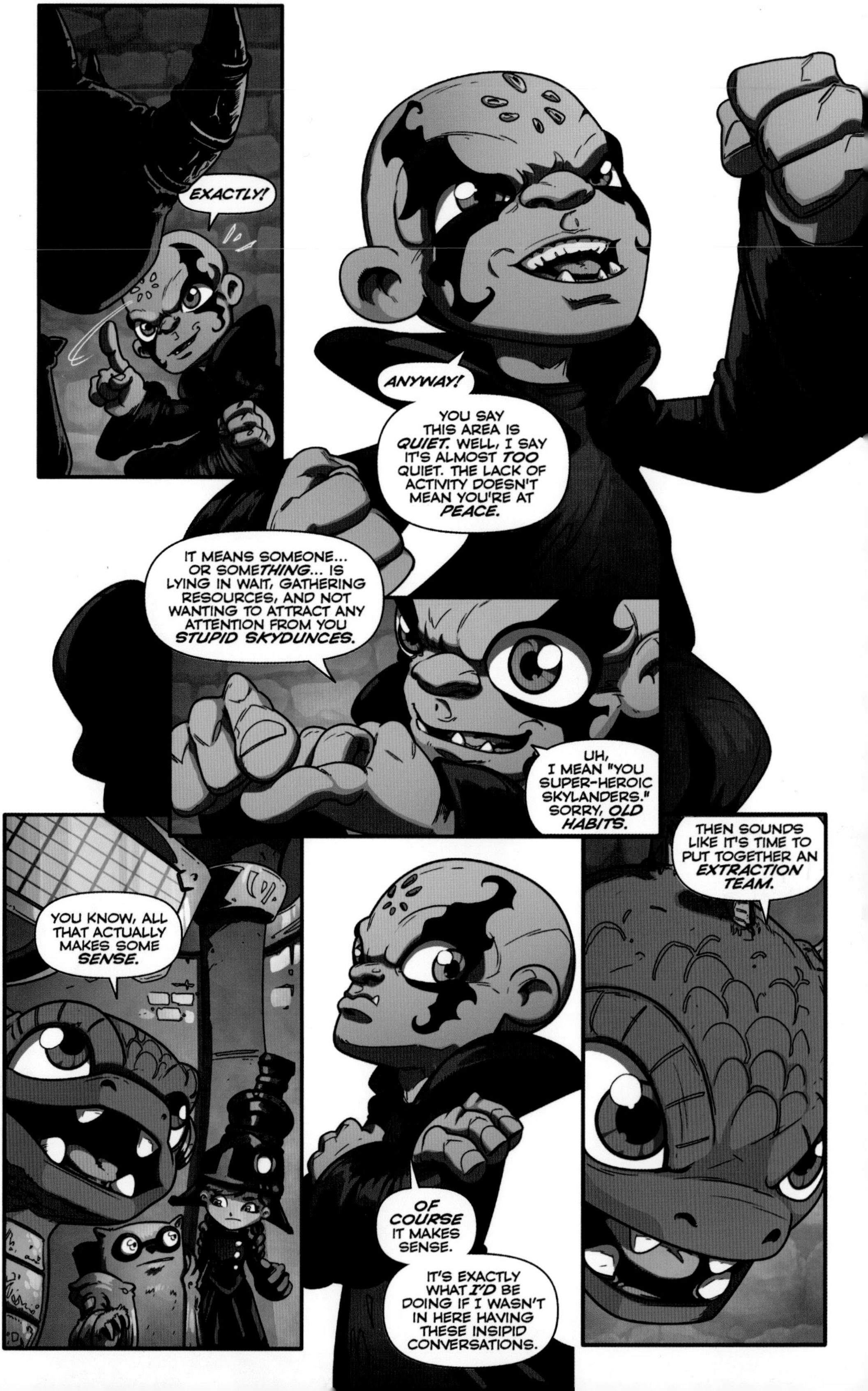
EXACTLY!
ANYWAY!
YOU SAY THIS AREA IS QUIET. WELL, I SAY IT'S ALMOST TOO QUIET. THE LACK OF ACTIVITY DOESN'T MEAN YOU'RE AT PEACE.
IT MEANS SOMEONE... OR SOMETHING... IS LYING IN WAIT, GATHERING RESOURCES, AND NOT WANTING TO ATTRACT ANY ATTENTION FROM YOU STUPID SKYDUNCES.
UH, I MEAN "YOU SUPER-HEROIC SKYLANDERS." SORRY, OLD HABITS.
YOU KNOW, ALL THAT ACTUALLY MAKES SOME SENSE.
OF COURSE IT MAKES SENSE.
IT'S EXACTLY WHAT I'D BE DOING IF I WASN'T IN HERE HAVING THESE INSIPID CONVERSATIONS.
THEN SOUNDS LIKE IT'S TIME TO PUT TOGETHER AN EXTRACTION TEAM.

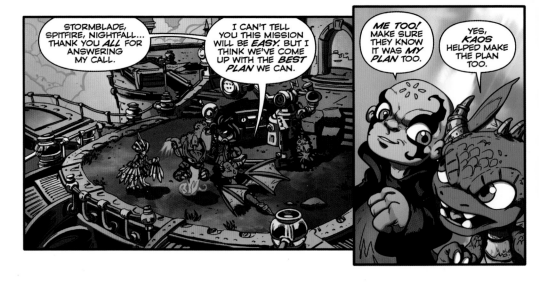

STORMBLADE, SPITFIRE, NIGHTFALL... THANK YOU *ALL* FOR ANSWERING MY CALL.

I CAN'T TELL YOU THIS MISSION WILL BE *EASY.* BUT I THINK WE'VE COME UP WITH THE *BEST PLAN* WE CAN.

ME TOO! MAKE SURE THEY KNOW IT WAS *MY PLAN* TOO.

YES, *KAOS* HELPED MAKE THE PLAN TOO.

I'M *SO* EXCITED TO BE GOING ON AN ACTUAL SKYLANDER MISSION!

SETTLE DOWN, STORMBLADE.

NIGHTFALL'S RIGHT. THIS MISSION COULD BE *DANGEROUS.*

I'VE ALREADY GIVEN YOU THE LAST KNOWN *LOCATION* OF BUZZ'S ELITE. YOUR MISSION IS TO BRING BACK THE *TEAM,* PLUS ANY *INFORMATION* YOU CAN FIND.

THIS ISN'T ABOUT STARTING A *FIGHT.* GET *THEM* HOME, AND GET *YOURSELVES* HOME SAFE.

ALL RIGHT, *SUPERCHARGERS,* YOU HEARD THE DRAGON...

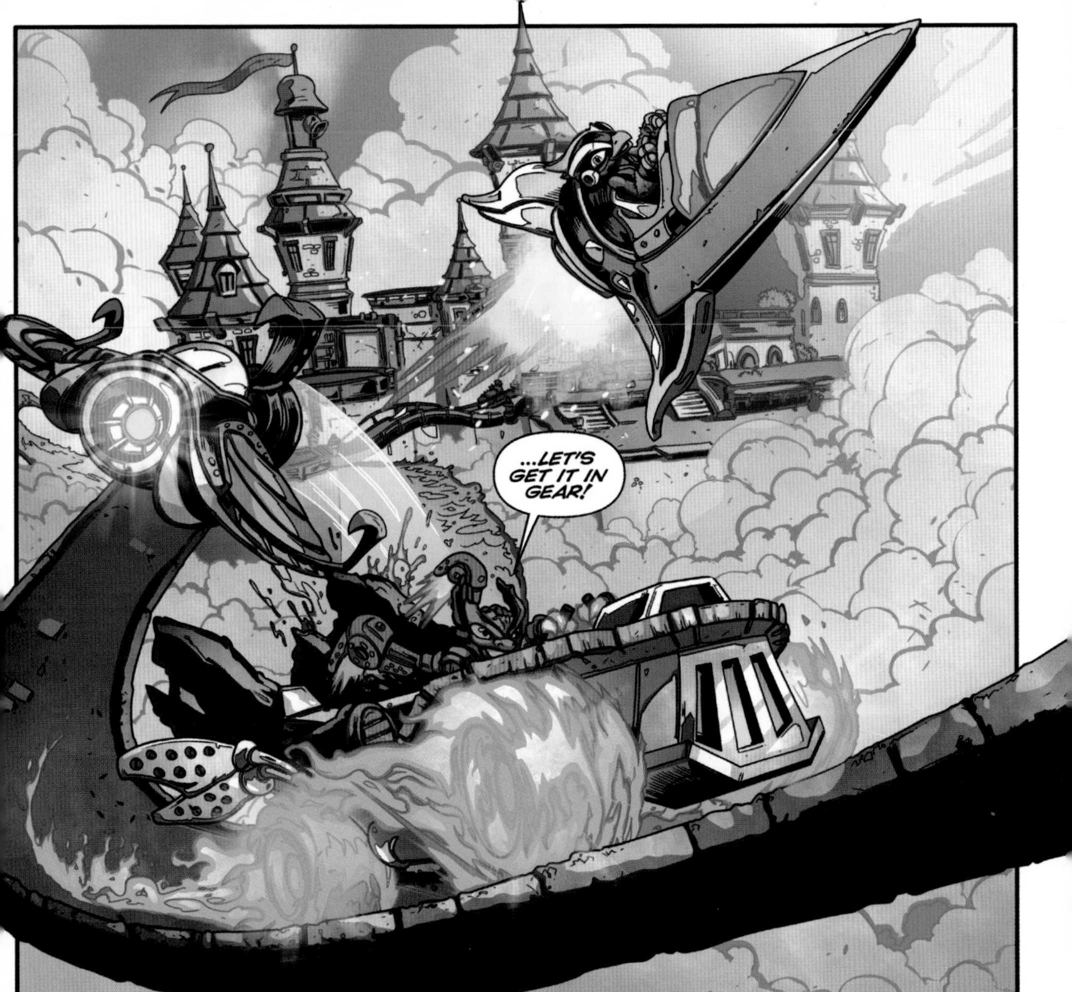
...LET'S GET IT IN GEAR!

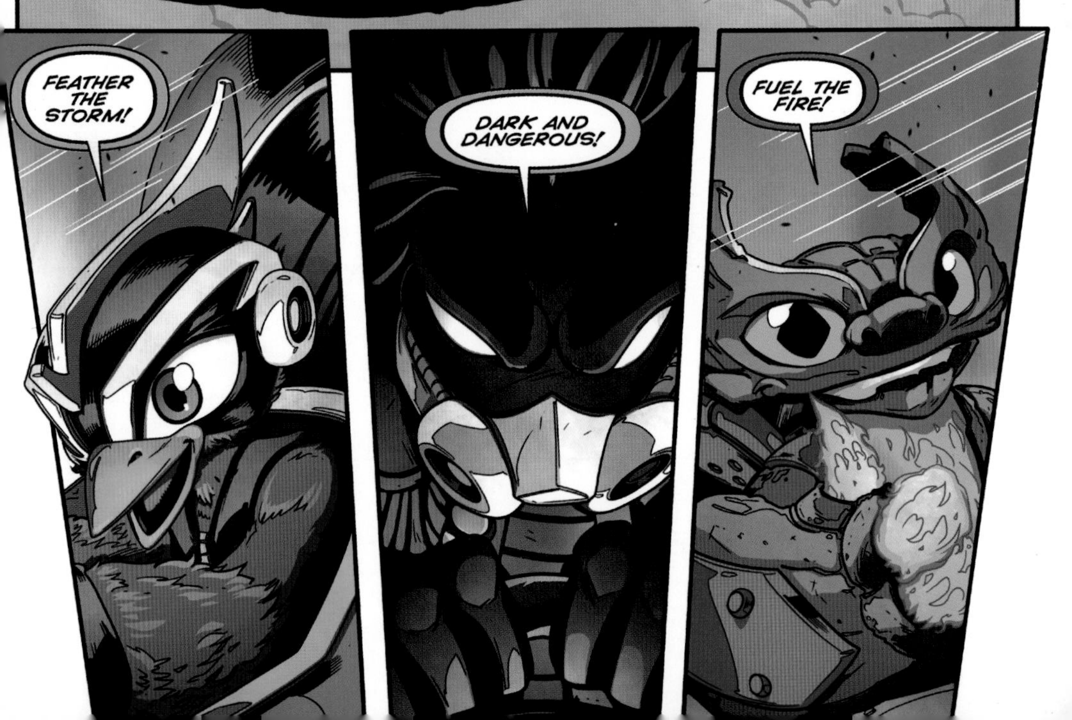
FEATHER THE STORM!
DARK AND DANGEROUS!
FUEL THE FIRE!

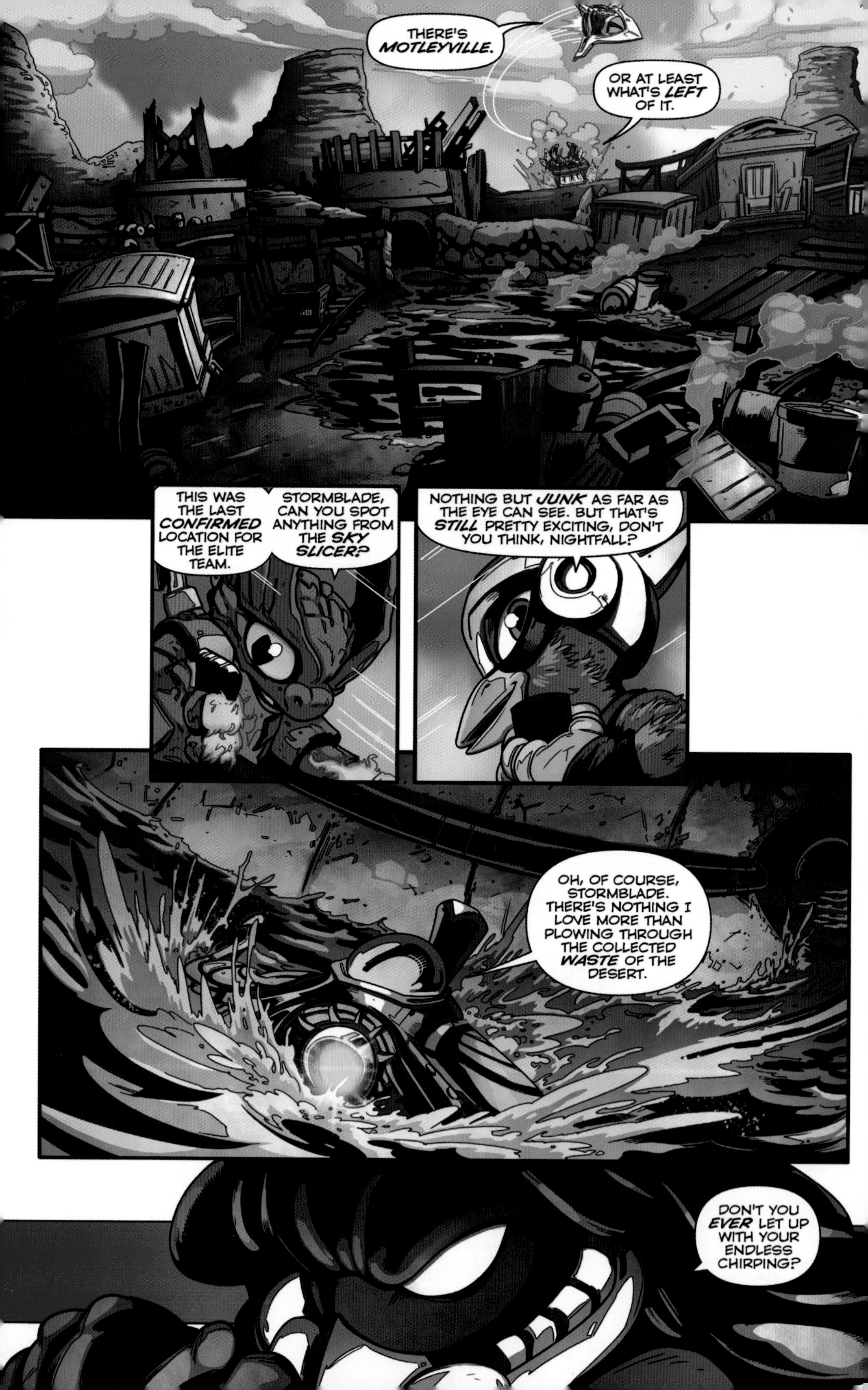

THERE'S *MOTLEYVILLE.*
OR AT LEAST WHAT'S *LEFT* OF IT.
THIS WAS THE LAST *CONFIRMED* LOCATION FOR THE ELITE TEAM.
STORMBLADE, CAN YOU SPOT ANYTHING FROM THE *SKY SLICER?*
NOTHING BUT *JUNK* AS FAR AS THE EYE CAN SEE. BUT THAT'S *STILL* PRETTY EXCITING, DON'T YOU THINK, NIGHTFALL?
OH, OF COURSE, STORMBLADE. THERE'S NOTHING I LOVE MORE THAN PLOWING THROUGH THE COLLECTED *WASTE* OF THE DESERT.
DON'T YOU *EVER* LET UP WITH YOUR ENDLESS CHIRPING?

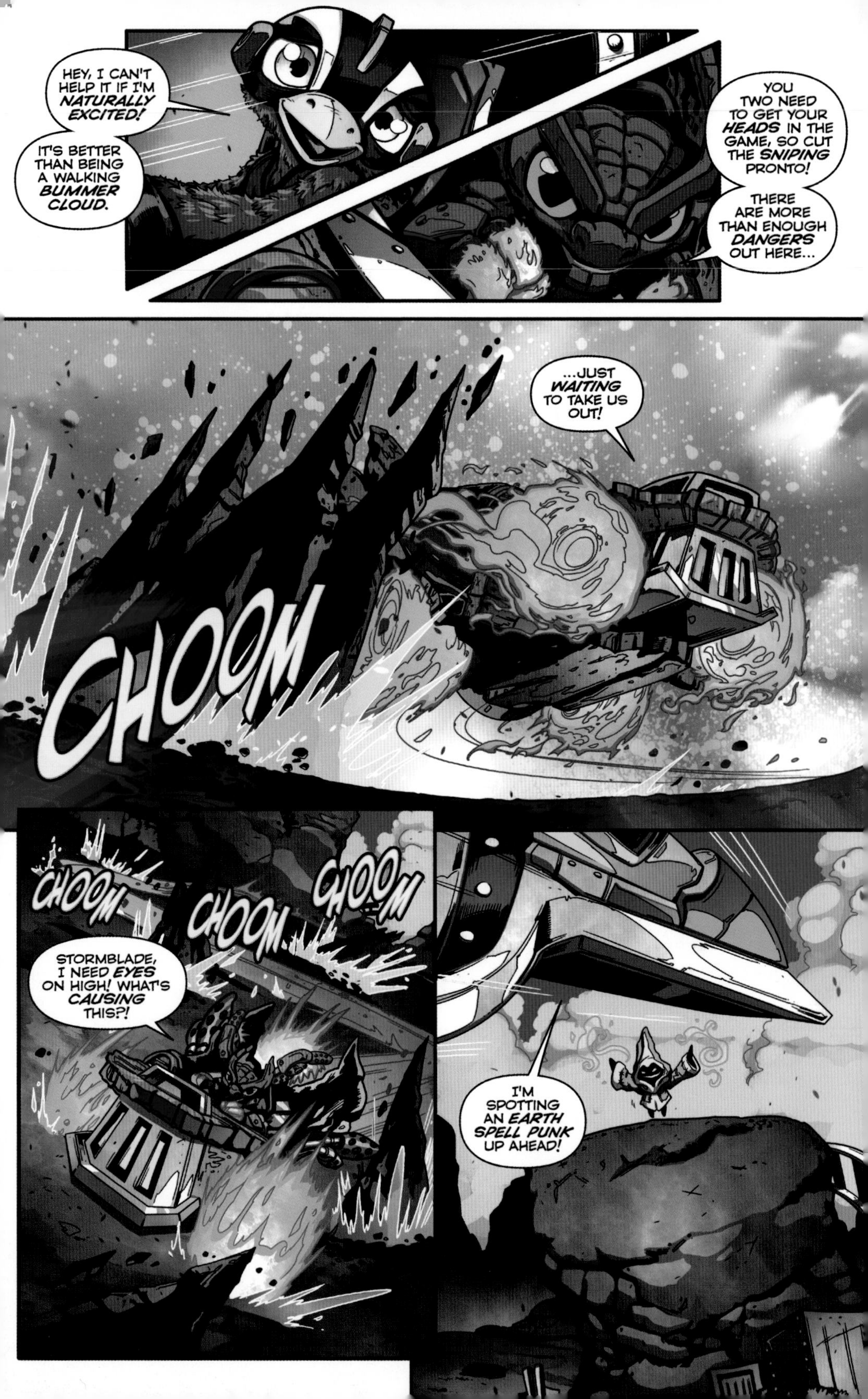
HEY, I CAN'T HELP IT IF I'M NATURALLY EXCITED!
IT'S BETTER THAN BEING A WALKING BUMMER CLOUD.
YOU TWO NEED TO GET YOUR HEADS IN THE GAME, SO CUT THE SNIPING PRONTO!
THERE ARE MORE THAN ENOUGH DANGERS OUT HERE...
...JUST WAITING TO TAKE US OUT!
CHOOM
CHOOM
CHOOM
CHOOM
STORMBLADE, I NEED EYES ON HIGH! WHAT'S CAUSING THIS?!
I'M SPOTTING AN EARTH SPELL PUNK UP AHEAD!

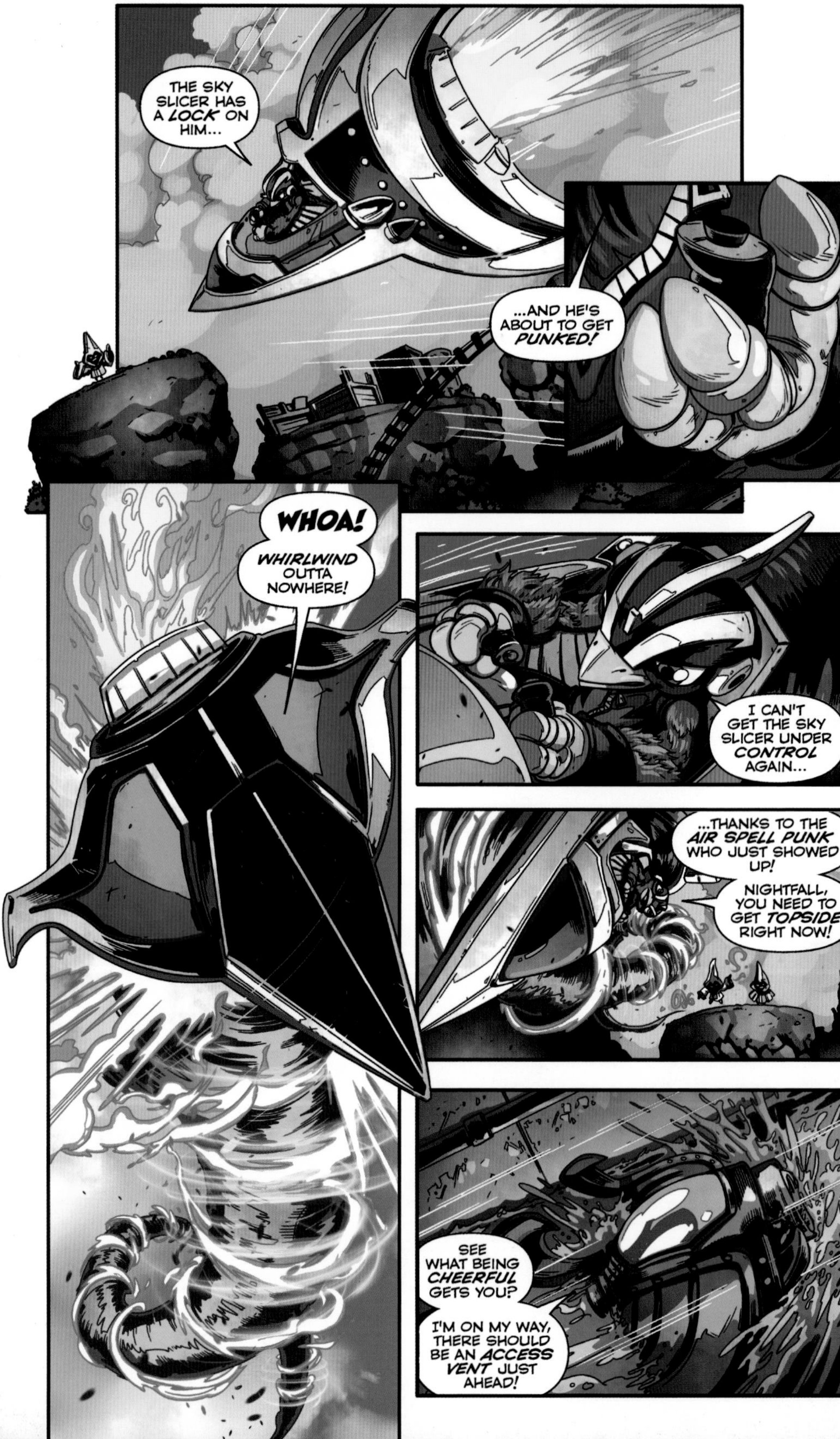
THE SKY SLICER HAS A LOCK ON HIM...
...AND HE'S ABOUT TO GET PUNKED!
WHOA!
WHIRLWIND OUTTA NOWHERE!
I CAN'T GET THE SKY SLICER UNDER CONTROL AGAIN...
...THANKS TO THE AIR SPELL PUNK WHO JUST SHOWED UP!
NIGHTFALL, YOU NEED TO GET TOPSIDE RIGHT NOW!
SEE WHAT BEING CHEERFUL GETS YOU?
I'M ON MY WAY, THERE SHOULD BE AN ACCESS VENT JUST AHEAD!

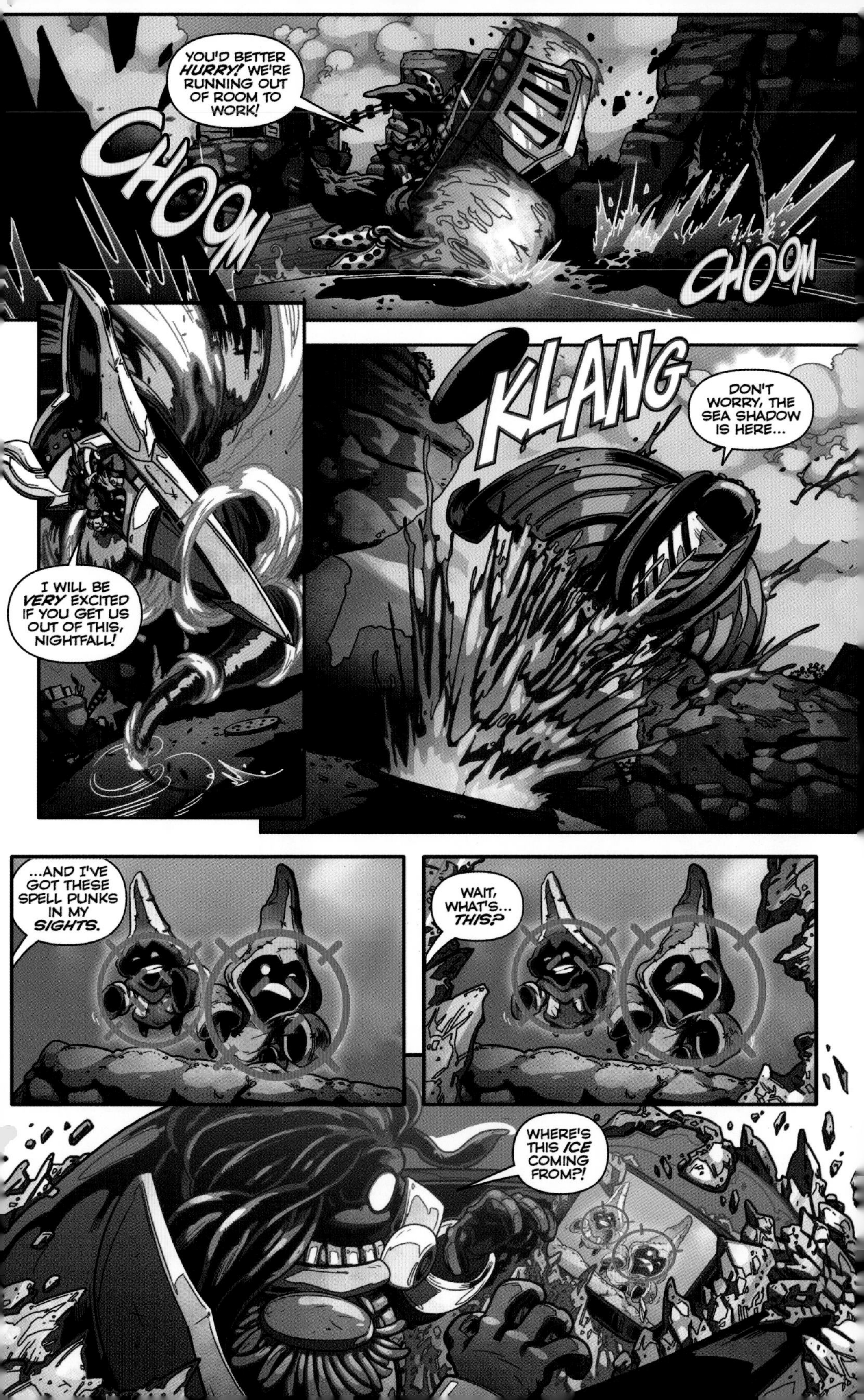

YOU'D BETTER HURRY! WE'RE RUNNING OUT OF ROOM TO WORK!
CHOOM
CHOOM
KLANG
DON'T WORRY, THE SEA SHADOW IS HERE...
I WILL BE VERY EXCITED IF YOU GET US OUT OF THIS, NIGHTFALL!
...AND I'VE GOT THESE SPELL PUNKS IN MY SIGHTS.
WAIT, WHAT'S... THIS?
WHERE'S THIS ICE COMING FROM?!

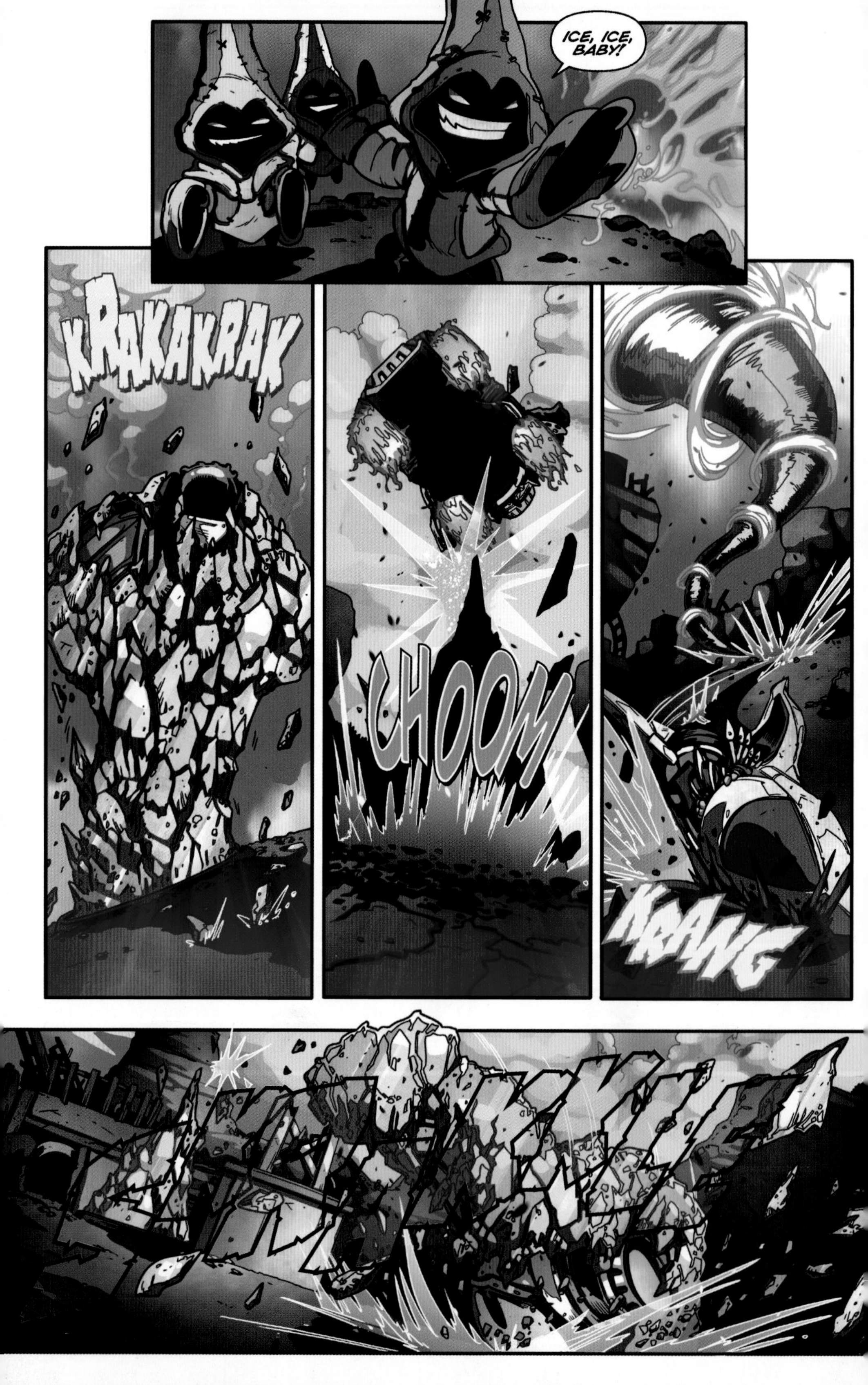
ICE, ICE, BABY!
KRAKAKRAK
CHOOM
KRANG

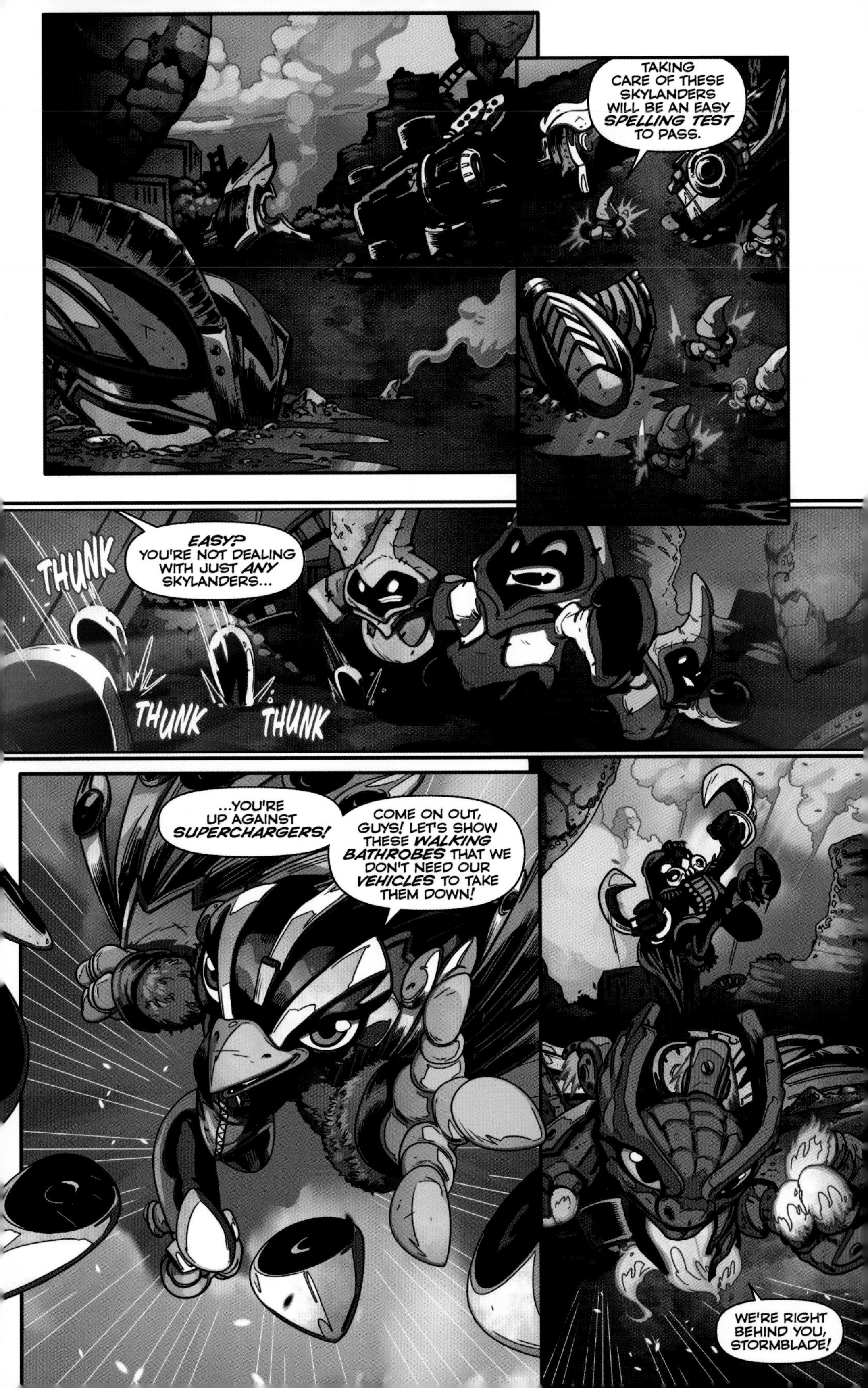
TAKING CARE OF THESE SKYLANDERS WILL BE AN EASY SPELLING TEST TO PASS.
THUNK
EASY? YOU'RE NOT DEALING WITH JUST ANY SKYLANDERS...
THUNK
THUNK
...YOU'RE UP AGAINST SUPERCHARGERS!
COME ON OUT, GUYS! LET'S SHOW THESE WALKING BATHROBES THAT WE DON'T NEED OUR VEHICLES TO TAKE THEM DOWN!
WE'RE RIGHT BEHIND YOU, STORMBLADE!

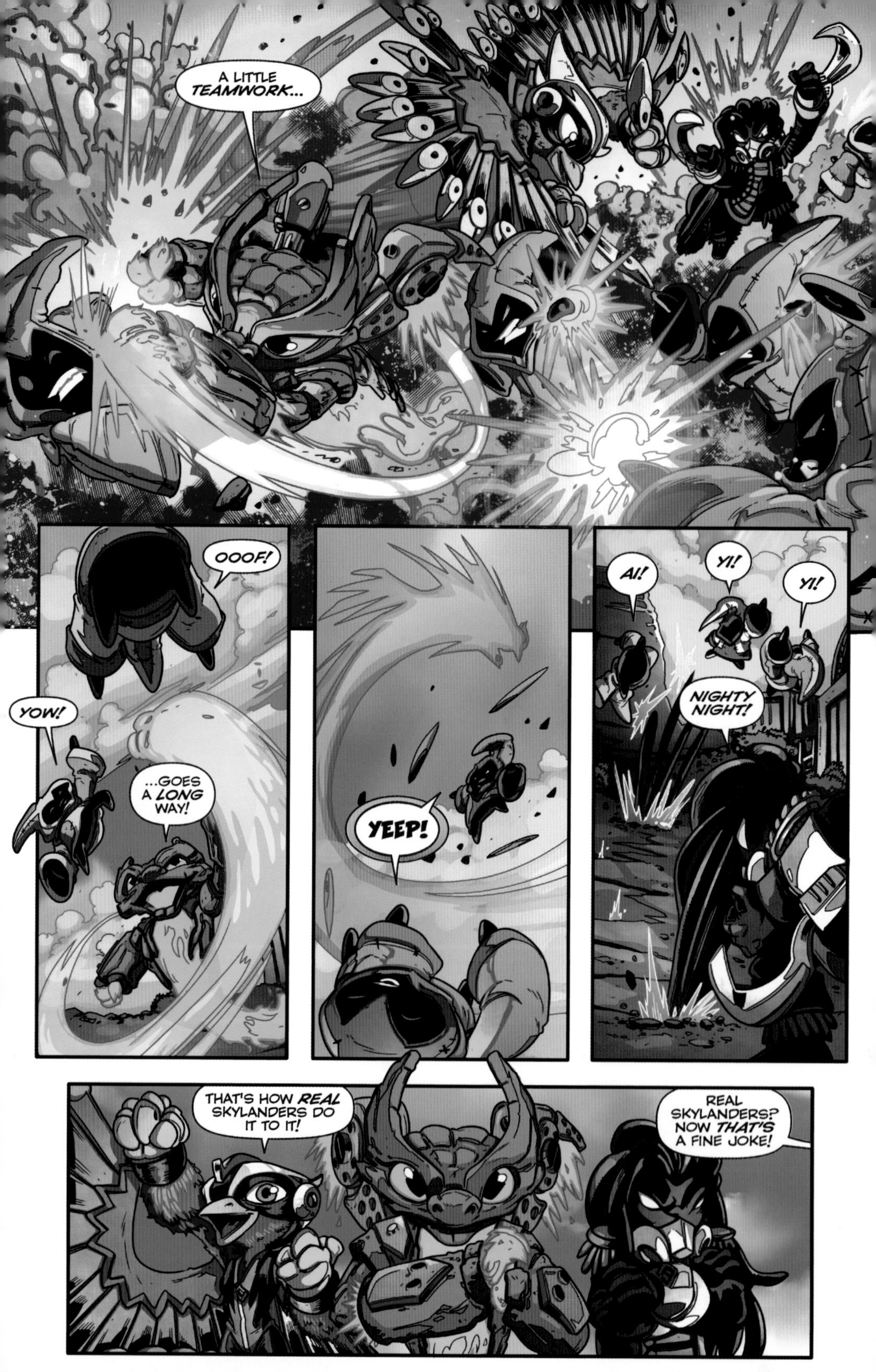
A LITTLE TEAMWORK...
OOOF!
YOW!
...GOES A LONG WAY!
YEEP!
AI!
YI!
YI!
NIGHTY NIGHT!
THAT'S HOW REAL SKYLANDERS DO IT TO IT!
REAL SKYLANDERS? NOW THAT'S A FINE JOKE!

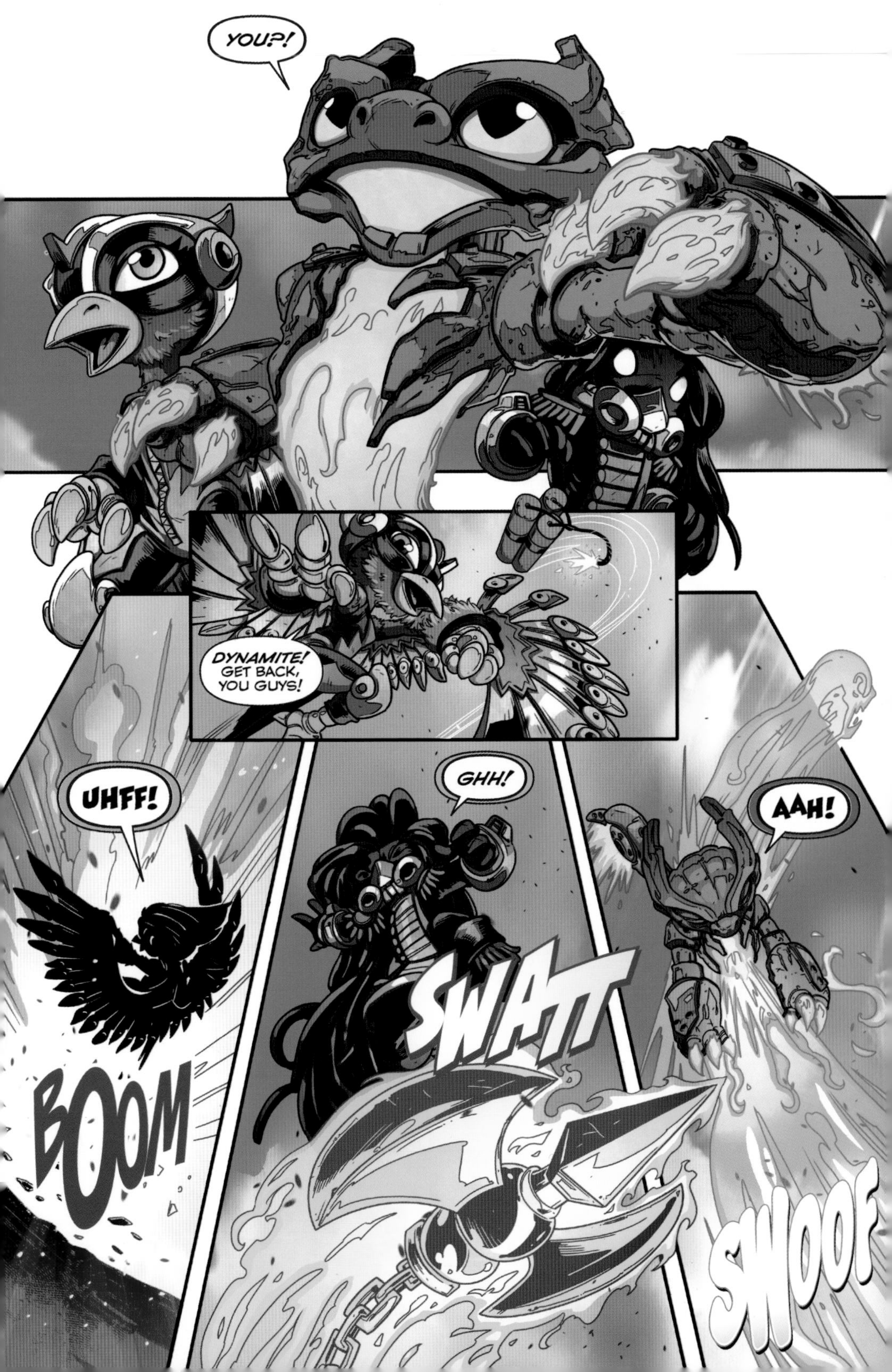
YOU?!
DYNAMITE! GET BACK, YOU GUYS!
UHFF!
BOOM
GHH!
SWATT
AAH!
SWOOF

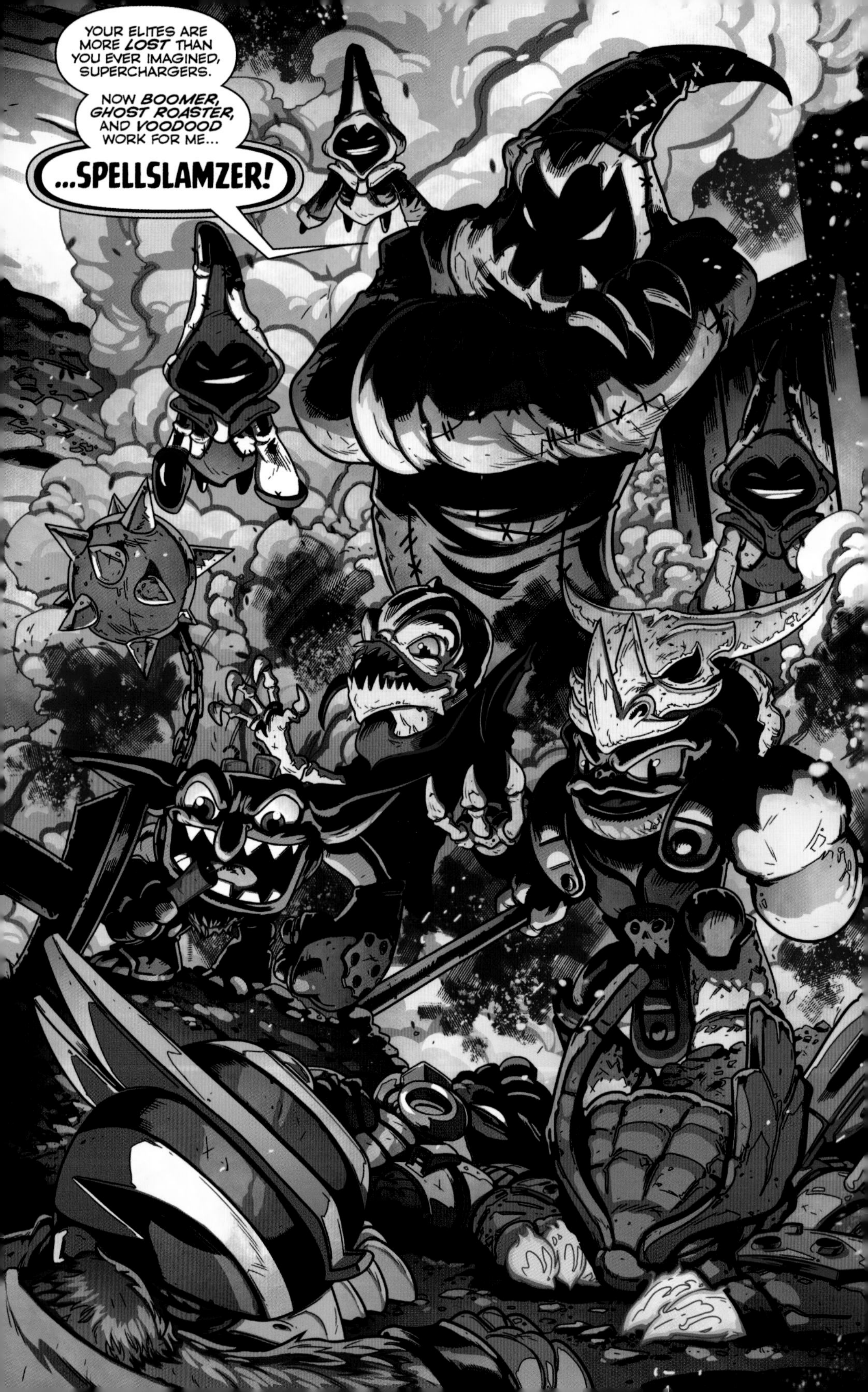
YOUR ELITES ARE MORE *LOST* THAN YOU EVER IMAGINED, SUPERCHARGERS.
NOW *BOOMER, GHOST ROASTER,* AND *VOODOOD* WORK FOR ME...
...SPELLSLAMZER!

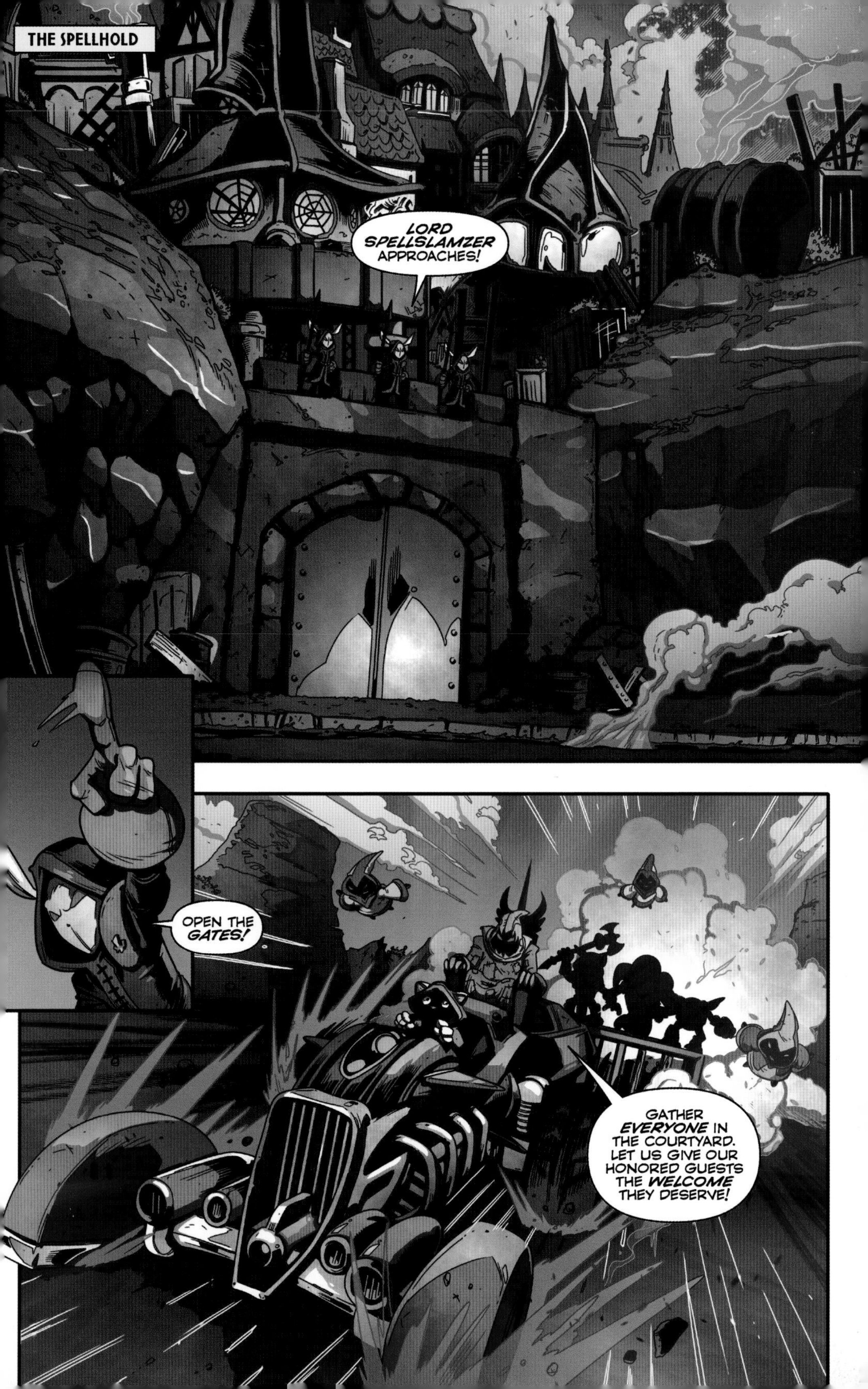
THE SPELLHOLD
LORD SPELLSLAMZER APPROACHES!
OPEN THE GATES!
GATHER EVERYONE IN THE COURTYARD. LET US GIVE OUR HONORED GUESTS THE WELCOME THEY DESERVE!

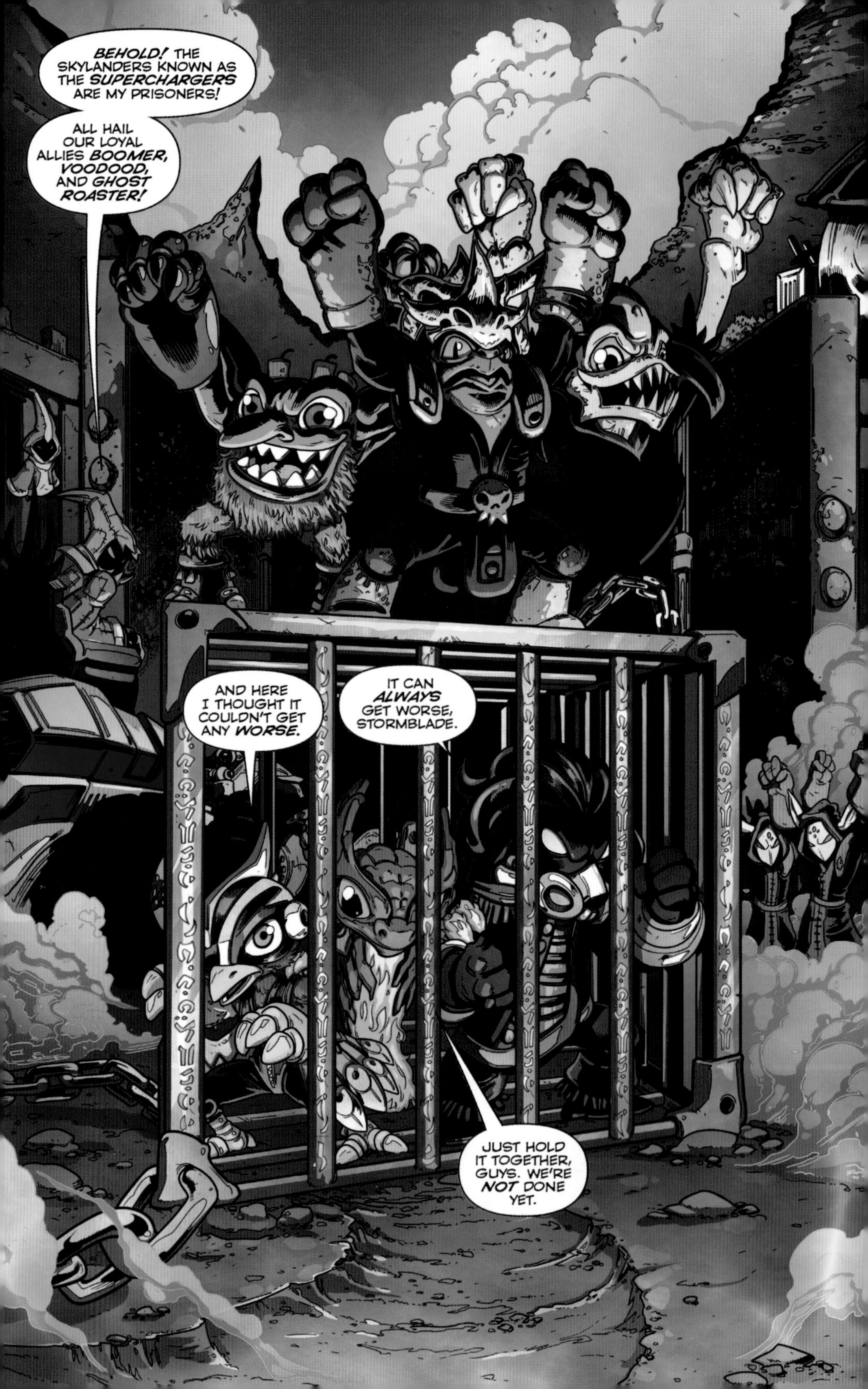
BEHOLD! THE SKYLANDERS KNOWN AS THE SUPERCHARGERS ARE MY PRISONERS!
ALL HAIL OUR LOYAL ALLIES BOOMER, VOODOOD, AND GHOST ROASTER!
AND HERE I THOUGHT IT COULDN'T GET ANY WORSE.
IT CAN ALWAYS GET WORSE, STORMBLADE.
JUST HOLD IT TOGETHER, GUYS. WE'RE NOT DONE YET.

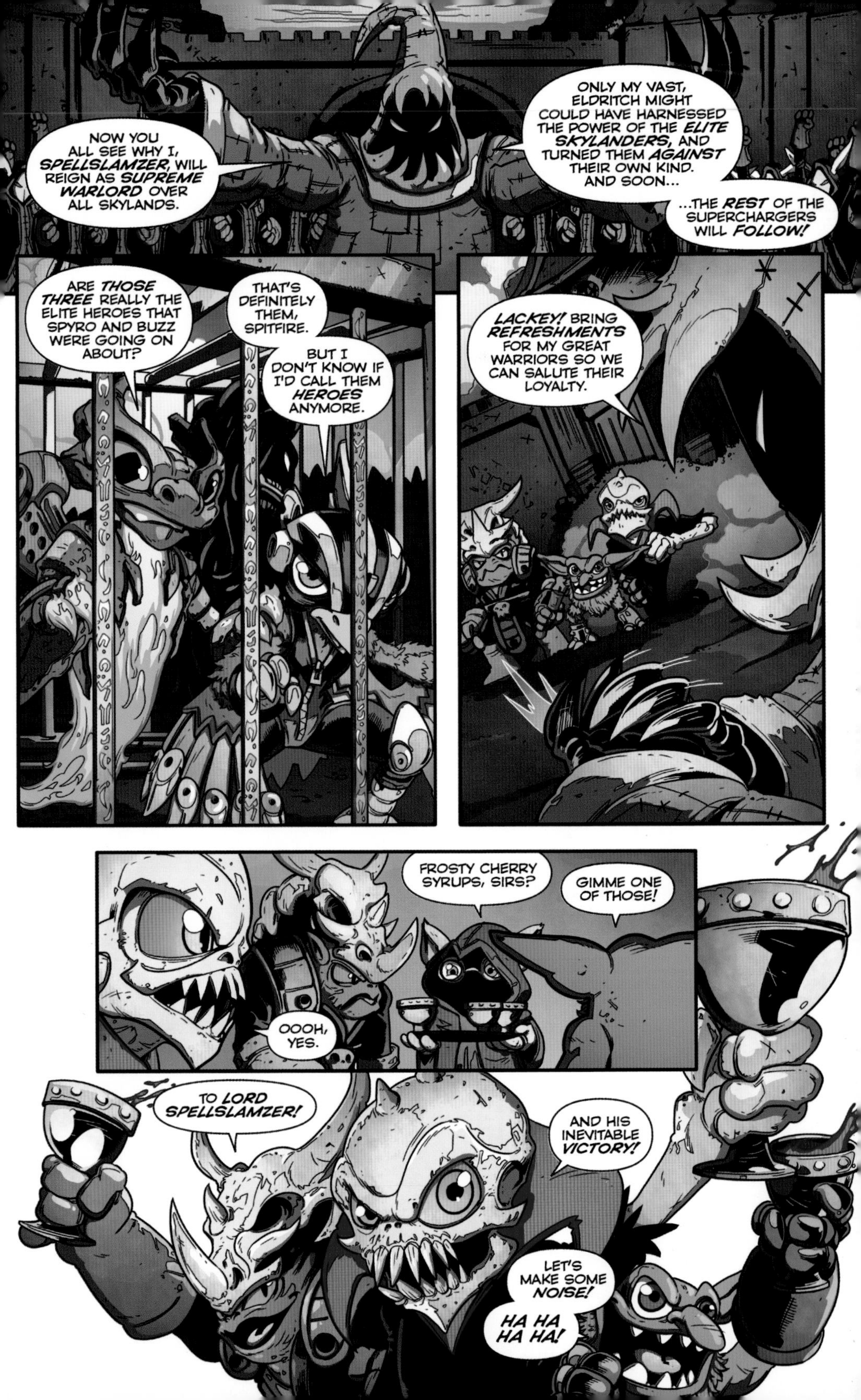
NOW YOU ALL SEE WHY I, SPELLSLAMZER, WILL REIGN AS SUPREME WARLORD OVER ALL SKYLANDS.
ONLY MY VAST, ELDRITCH MIGHT COULD HAVE HARNESSED THE POWER OF THE ELITE SKYLANDERS, AND TURNED THEM AGAINST THEIR OWN KIND. AND SOON...
...THE REST OF THE SUPERCHARGERS WILL FOLLOW!
ARE THOSE THREE REALLY THE ELITE HEROES THAT SPYRO AND BUZZ WERE GOING ON ABOUT?
THAT'S DEFINITELY THEM, SPITFIRE.
BUT I DON'T KNOW IF I'D CALL THEM HEROES ANYMORE.
LACKEY! BRING REFRESHMENTS FOR MY GREAT WARRIORS SO WE CAN SALUTE THEIR LOYALTY.
FROSTY CHERRY SYRUPS, SIRS?
GIMME ONE OF THOSE!
OOOH, YES.
TO LORD SPELLSLAMZER!
AND HIS INEVITABLE VICTORY!
LET'S MAKE SOME NOISE!
HA HA HA HA!

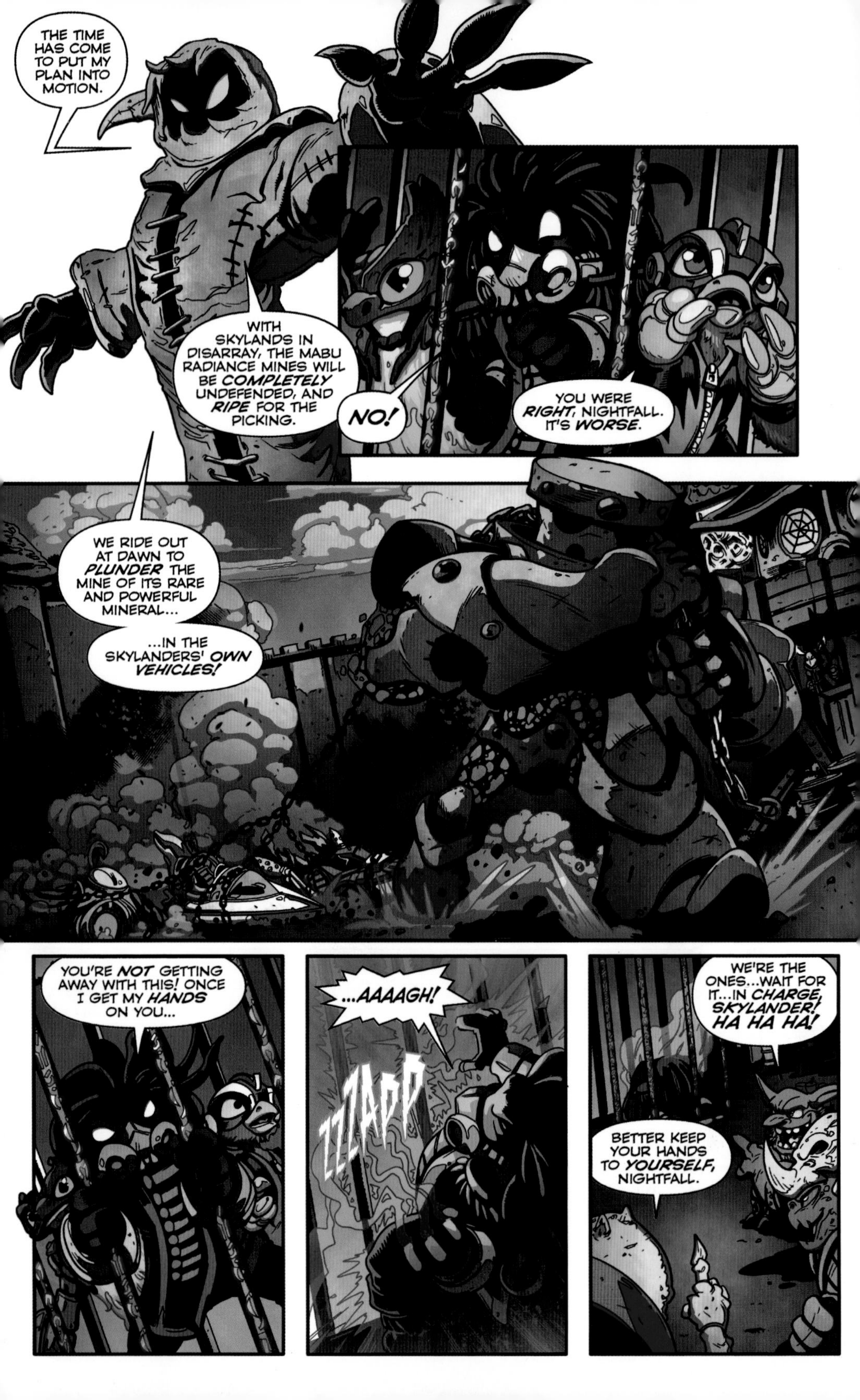
THE TIME HAS COME TO PUT MY PLAN INTO MOTION.
WITH SKYLANDS IN DISARRAY, THE MABU RADIANCE MINES WILL BE *COMPLETELY* UNDEFENDED, AND *RIPE* FOR THE PICKING.
NO!
YOU WERE *RIGHT*, NIGHTFALL. IT'S *WORSE*.
WE RIDE OUT AT DAWN TO *PLUNDER* THE MINE OF ITS RARE AND POWERFUL MINERAL...
...IN THE SKYLANDERS' *OWN VEHICLES!*
YOU'RE *NOT* GETTING AWAY WITH THIS! ONCE I GET MY *HANDS* ON YOU...
...AAAAGH!
ZZZAPP
WE'RE THE ONES...WAIT FOR IT...IN *CHARGE*, *SKYLANDER! HA HA HA!*
BETTER KEEP YOUR HANDS TO *YOURSELF*, NIGHTFALL.

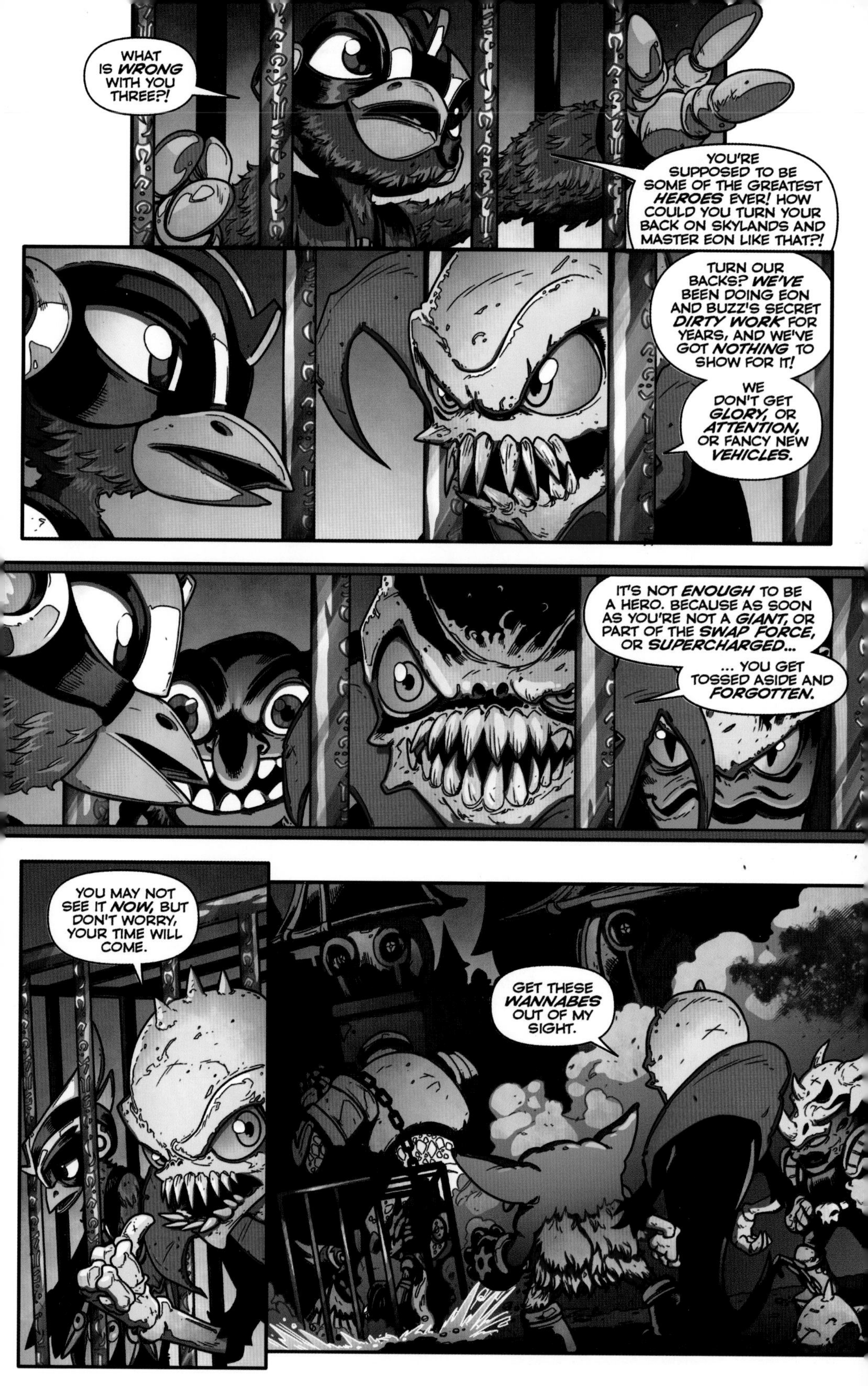
WHAT IS WRONG WITH YOU THREE?!
YOU'RE SUPPOSED TO BE SOME OF THE GREATEST HEROES EVER! HOW COULD YOU TURN YOUR BACK ON SKYLANDS AND MASTER EON LIKE THAT?!
TURN OUR BACKS? WE'VE BEEN DOING EON AND BUZZ'S SECRET DIRTY WORK FOR YEARS, AND WE'VE GOT NOTHING TO SHOW FOR IT!
WE DON'T GET GLORY, OR ATTENTION, OR FANCY NEW VEHICLES.
IT'S NOT ENOUGH TO BE A HERO. BECAUSE AS SOON AS YOU'RE NOT A GIANT, OR PART OF THE SWAP FORCE, OR SUPERCHARGED...
... YOU GET TOSSED ASIDE AND FORGOTTEN.
YOU MAY NOT SEE IT NOW, BUT DON'T WORRY, YOUR TIME WILL COME.
GET THESE WANNABES OUT OF MY SIGHT.

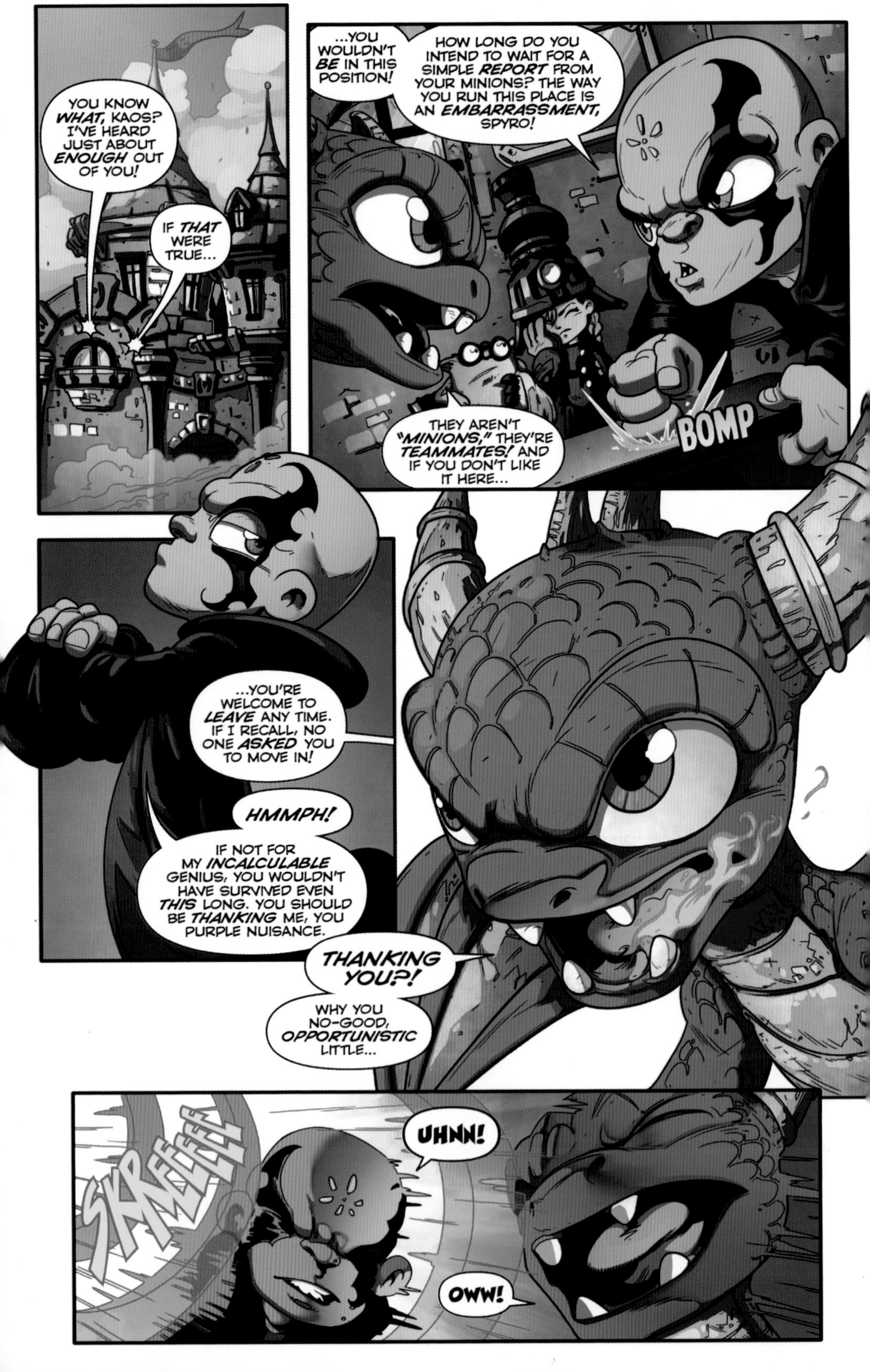

YOU KNOW WHAT, KAOS? I'VE HEARD JUST ABOUT ENOUGH OUT OF YOU!
IF THAT WERE TRUE...
...YOU WOULDN'T BE IN THIS POSITION!
HOW LONG DO YOU INTEND TO WAIT FOR A SIMPLE REPORT FROM YOUR MINIONS? THE WAY YOU RUN THIS PLACE IS AN EMBARRASSMENT, SPYRO!
BOMP
THEY AREN'T "MINIONS," THEY'RE TEAMMATES! AND IF YOU DON'T LIKE IT HERE...
...YOU'RE WELCOME TO LEAVE ANY TIME. IF I RECALL, NO ONE ASKED YOU TO MOVE IN!
HMMPH!
IF NOT FOR MY INCALCULABLE GENIUS, YOU WOULDN'T HAVE SURVIVED EVEN THIS LONG. YOU SHOULD BE THANKING ME, YOU PURPLE NUISANCE.
THANKING YOU?!
WHY YOU NO-GOOD, OPPORTUNISTIC LITTLE...
SKREEEEE
UHNN!
OWW!

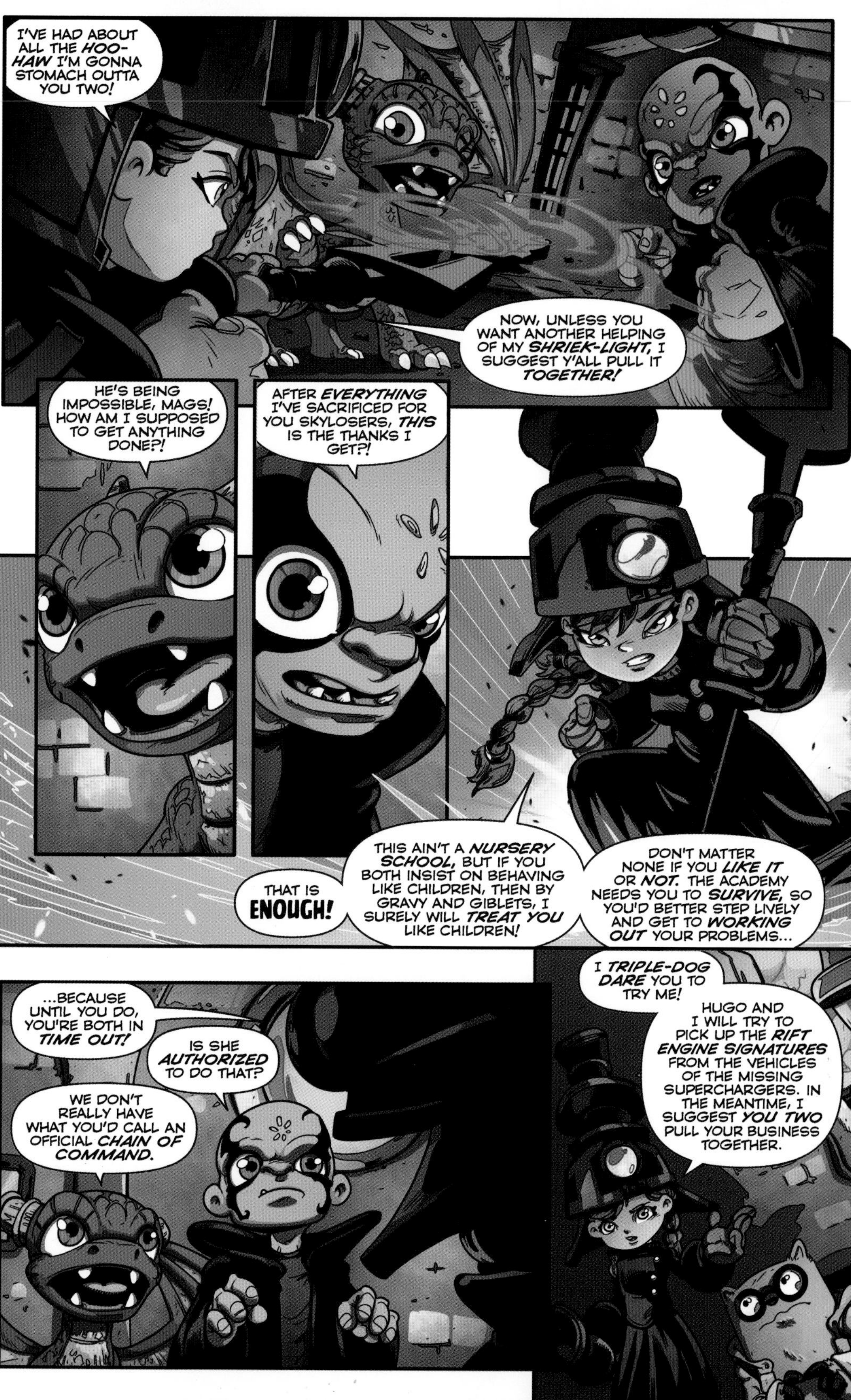
I'VE HAD ABOUT ALL THE HOO-HAW I'M GONNA STOMACH OUTTA YOU TWO!
NOW, UNLESS YOU WANT ANOTHER HELPING OF MY SHRIEK-LIGHT, I SUGGEST Y'ALL PULL IT TOGETHER!
HE'S BEING IMPOSSIBLE, MAGS! HOW AM I SUPPOSED TO GET ANYTHING DONE?!
AFTER EVERYTHING I'VE SACRIFICED FOR YOU SKYLOSERS, THIS IS THE THANKS I GET?!
THAT IS ENOUGH!
THIS AIN'T A NURSERY SCHOOL, BUT IF YOU BOTH INSIST ON BEHAVING LIKE CHILDREN, THEN BY GRAVY AND GIBLETS, I SURELY WILL TREAT YOU LIKE CHILDREN!
DON'T MATTER NONE IF YOU LIKE IT OR NOT. THE ACADEMY NEEDS YOU TO SURVIVE, SO YOU'D BETTER STEP LIVELY AND GET TO WORKING OUT YOUR PROBLEMS...
...BECAUSE UNTIL YOU DO, YOU'RE BOTH IN TIME OUT!
IS SHE AUTHORIZED TO DO THAT?
WE DON'T REALLY HAVE WHAT YOU'D CALL AN OFFICIAL CHAIN OF COMMAND.
I TRIPLE-DOG DARE YOU TO TRY ME!
HUGO AND I WILL TRY TO PICK UP THE RIFT ENGINE SIGNATURES FROM THE VEHICLES OF THE MISSING SUPERCHARGERS. IN THE MEANTIME, I SUGGEST YOU TWO PULL YOUR BUSINESS TOGETHER.

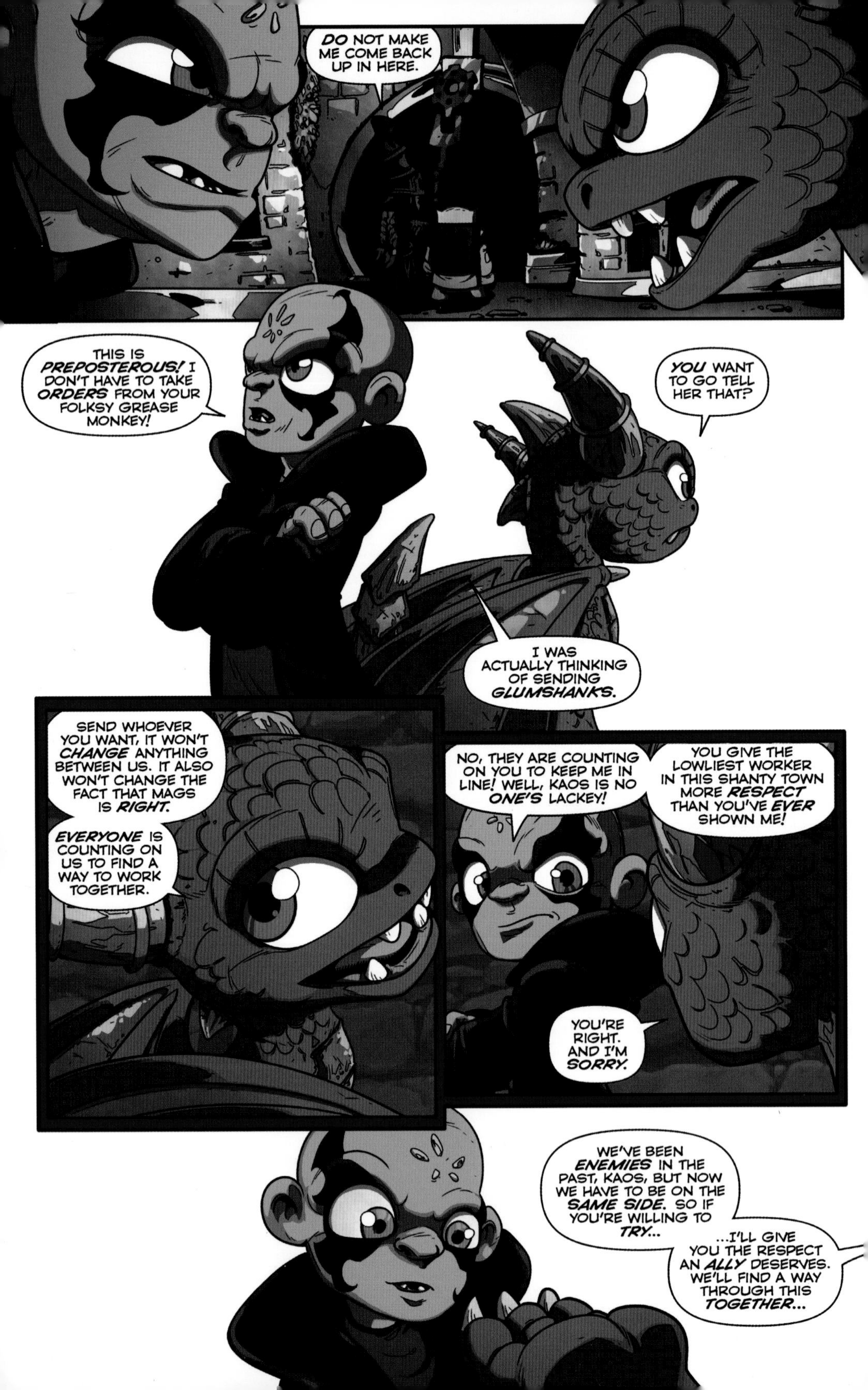
DO NOT MAKE ME COME BACK UP IN HERE.
THIS IS PREPOSTEROUS! I DON'T HAVE TO TAKE ORDERS FROM YOUR FOLKSY GREASE MONKEY!
YOU WANT TO GO TELL HER THAT?
I WAS ACTUALLY THINKING OF SENDING GLUMSHANKS.
SEND WHOEVER YOU WANT, IT WON'T CHANGE ANYTHING BETWEEN US. IT ALSO WON'T CHANGE THE FACT THAT MAGS IS RIGHT.
EVERYONE IS COUNTING ON US TO FIND A WAY TO WORK TOGETHER.
NO, THEY ARE COUNTING ON YOU TO KEEP ME IN LINE! WELL, KAOS IS NO ONE'S LACKEY!
YOU GIVE THE LOWLIEST WORKER IN THIS SHANTY TOWN MORE RESPECT THAN YOU'VE EVER SHOWN ME!
YOU'RE RIGHT. AND I'M SORRY.
WE'VE BEEN ENEMIES IN THE PAST, KAOS, BUT NOW WE HAVE TO BE ON THE SAME SIDE. SO IF YOU'RE WILLING TO TRY...
...I'LL GIVE YOU THE RESPECT AN ALLY DESERVES. WE'LL FIND A WAY THROUGH THIS TOGETHER...

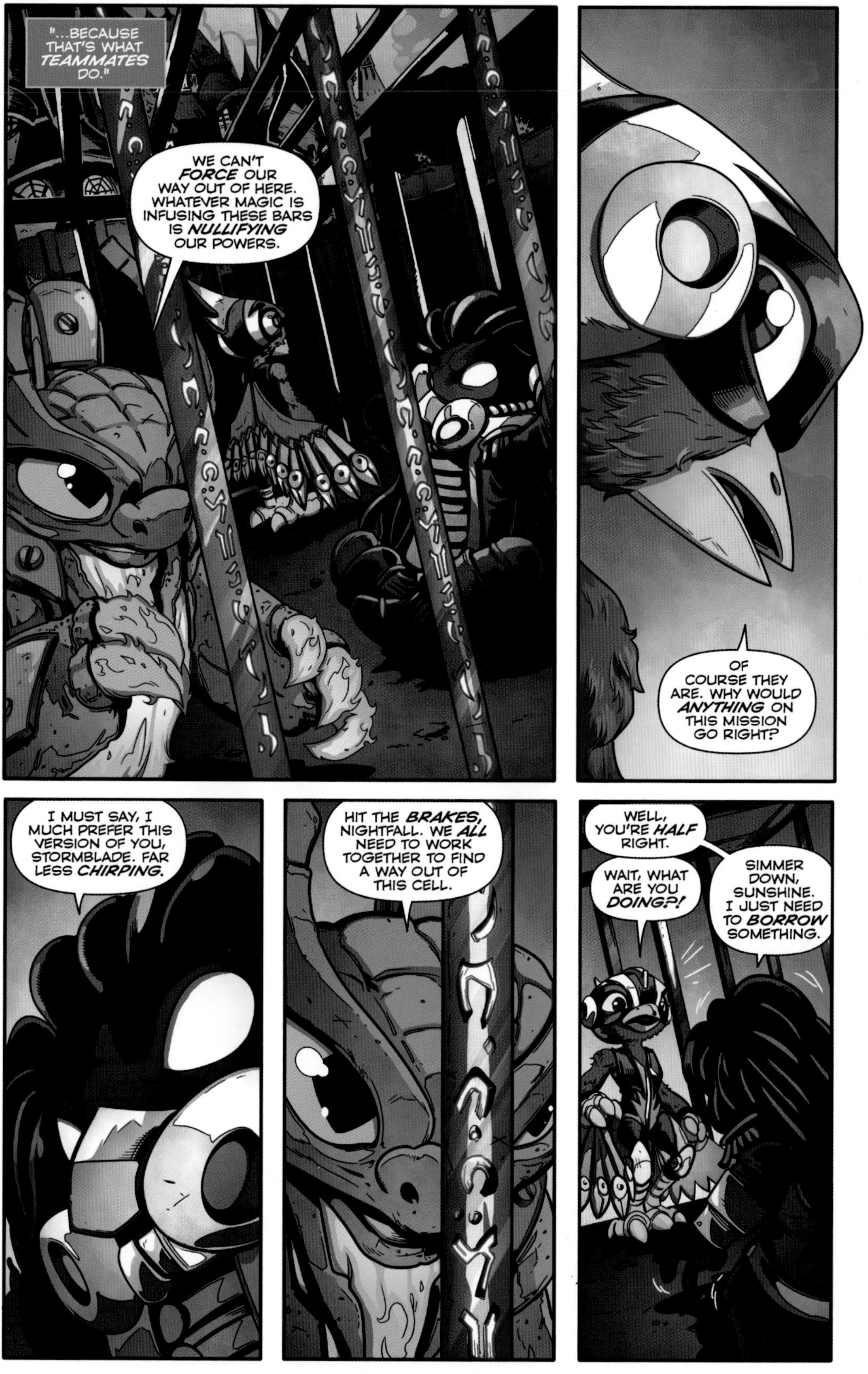
"...BECAUSE THAT'S WHAT *TEAMMATES* DO."
WE CAN'T *FORCE* OUR WAY OUT OF HERE. WHATEVER MAGIC IS INFUSING THESE BARS IS *NULLIFYING* OUR POWERS.
OF COURSE THEY ARE. WHY WOULD *ANYTHING* ON THIS MISSION GO RIGHT?
I MUST SAY, I MUCH PREFER THIS VERSION OF YOU, STORMBLADE. FAR LESS *CHIRPING*.
HIT THE *BRAKES*, NIGHTFALL. WE *ALL* NEED TO WORK TOGETHER TO FIND A WAY OUT OF THIS CELL.
WELL, YOU'RE *HALF* RIGHT.
WAIT, WHAT ARE YOU *DOING?!*
SIMMER DOWN, SUNSHINE. I JUST NEED TO *BORROW* SOMETHING.

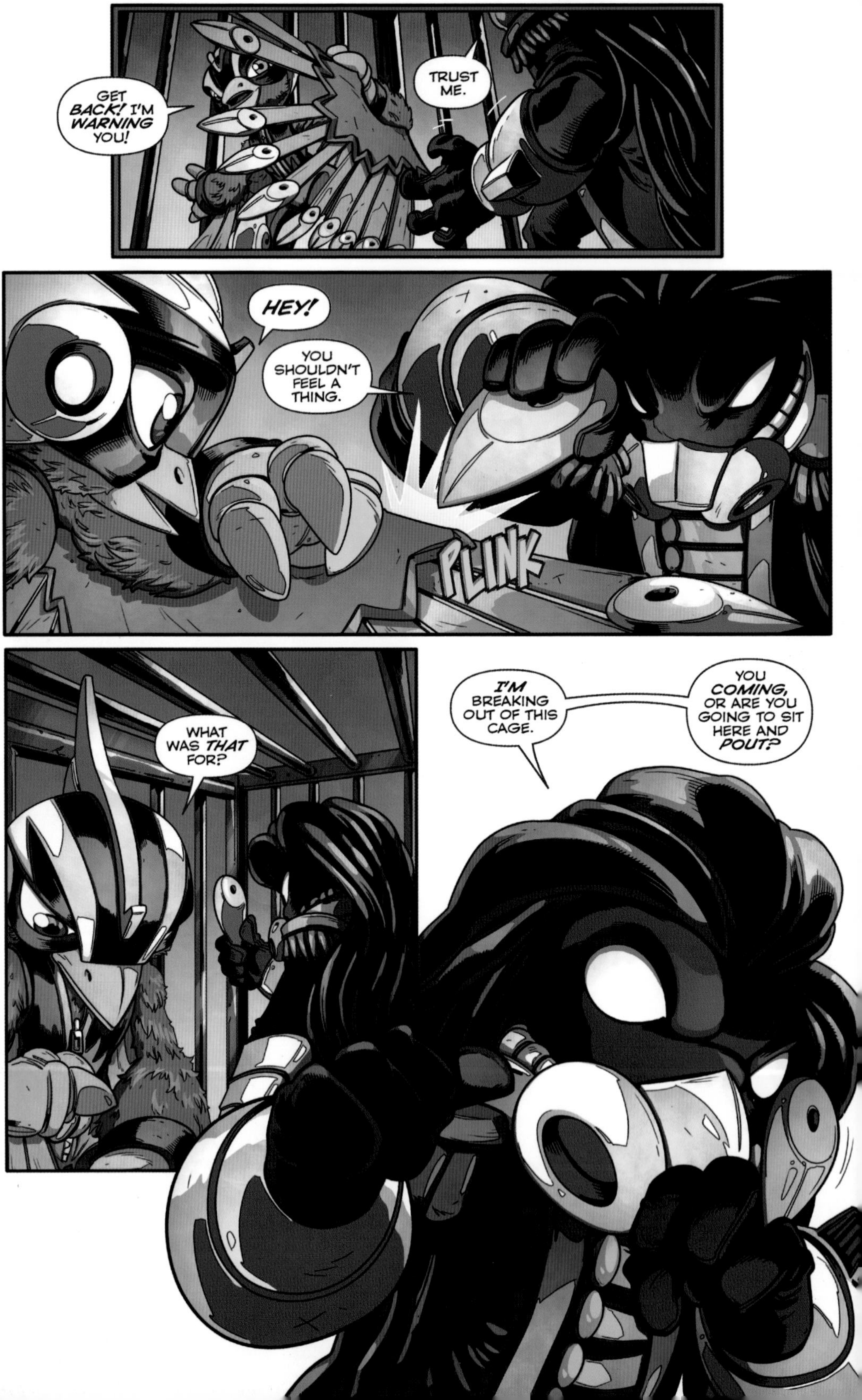
GET BACK! I'M WARNING YOU!
TRUST ME.
HEY!
YOU SHOULDN'T FEEL A THING.
PLINK
WHAT WAS THAT FOR?
I'M BREAKING OUT OF THIS CAGE.
YOU COMING, OR ARE YOU GOING TO SIT HERE AND POUT?

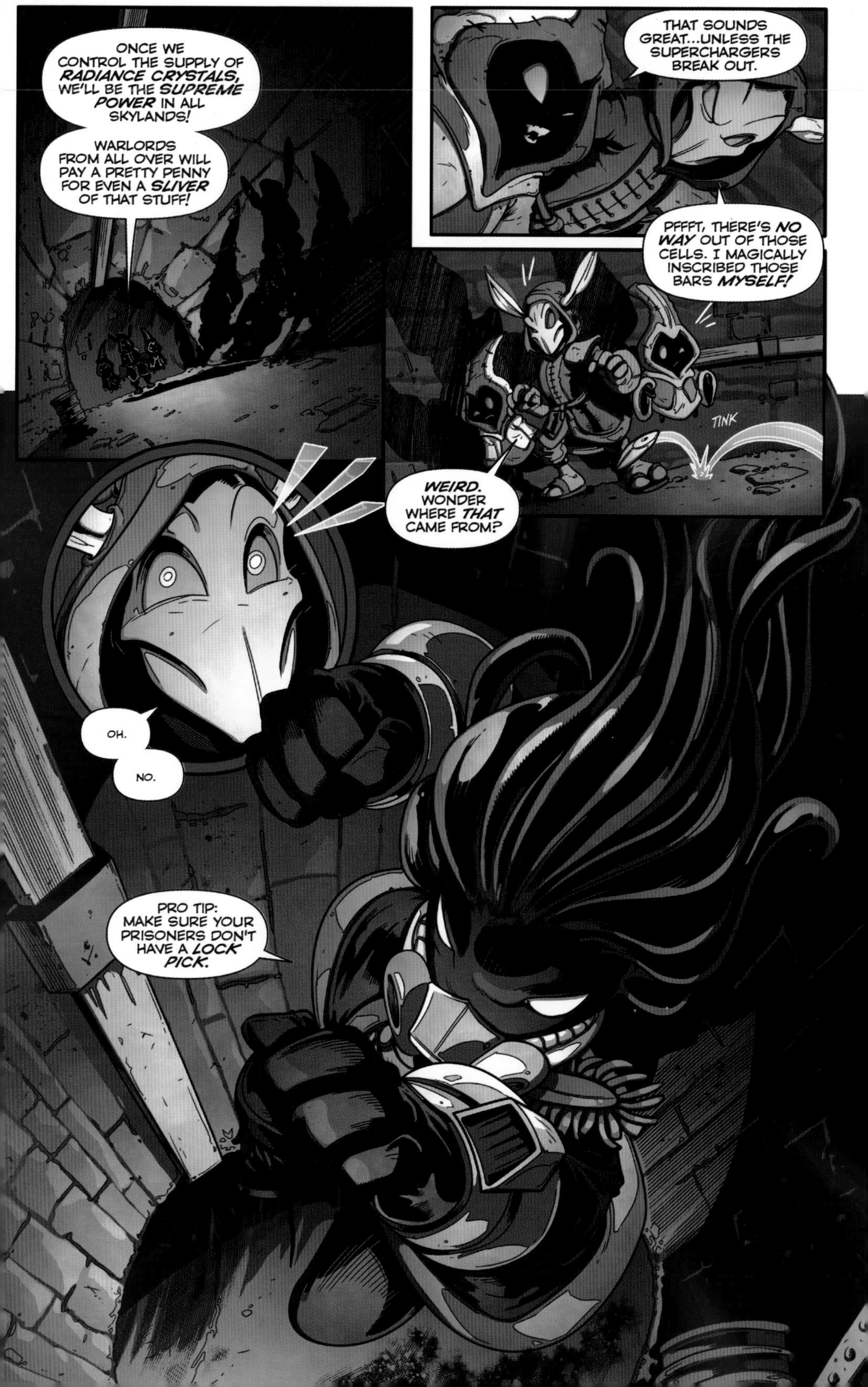

ONCE WE CONTROL THE SUPPLY OF RADIANCE CRYSTALS, WE'LL BE THE SUPREME POWER IN ALL SKYLANDS!
WARLORDS FROM ALL OVER WILL PAY A PRETTY PENNY FOR EVEN A SLIVER OF THAT STUFF!
THAT SOUNDS GREAT...UNLESS THE SUPERCHARGERS BREAK OUT.
PFFFT, THERE'S NO WAY OUT OF THOSE CELLS. I MAGICALLY INSCRIBED THOSE BARS MYSELF!
TINK
WEIRD. WONDER WHERE THAT CAME FROM?
OH.
NO.
PRO TIP: MAKE SURE YOUR PRISONERS DON'T HAVE A LOCK PICK.

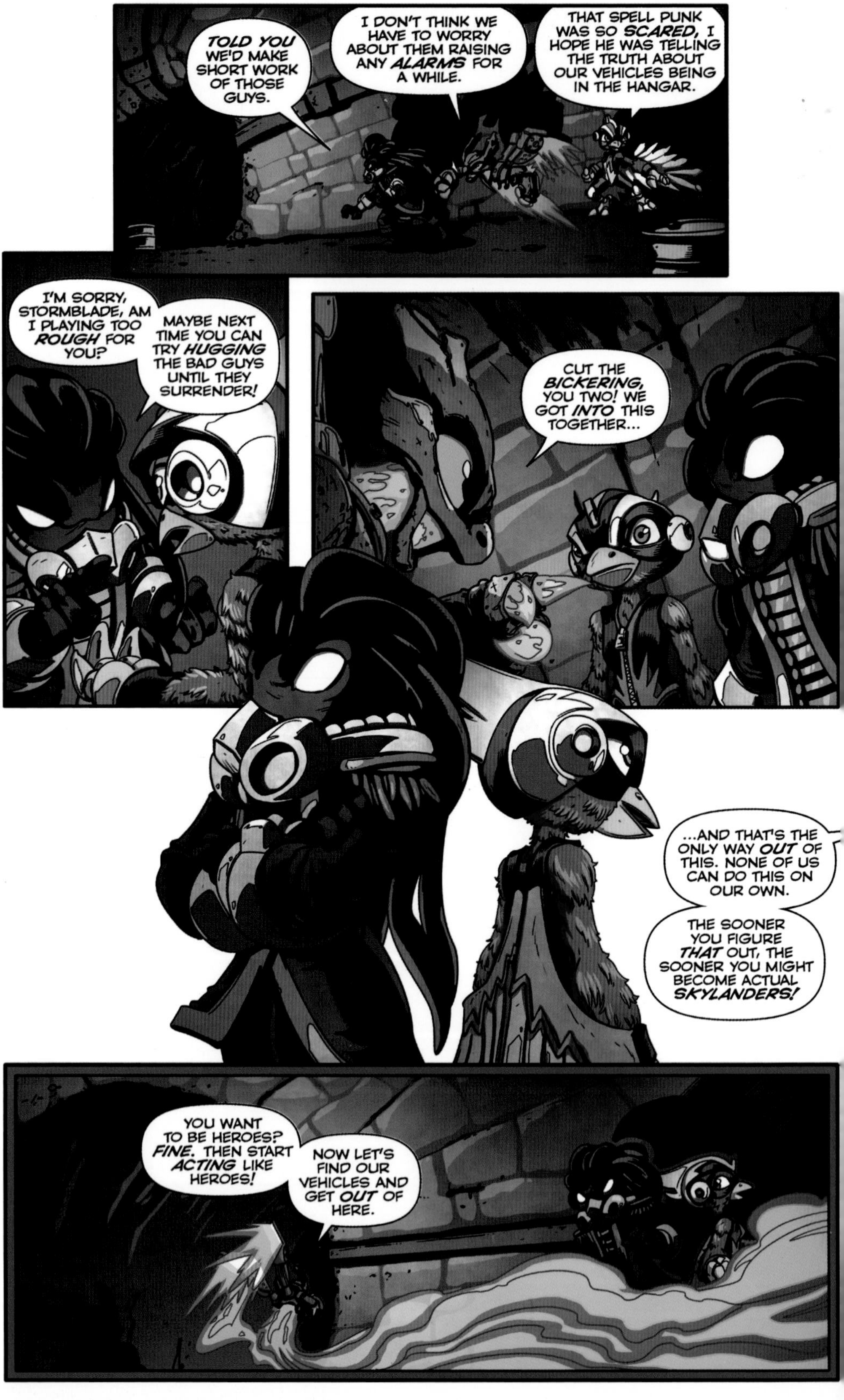

TOLD YOU WE'D MAKE SHORT WORK OF THOSE GUYS.
I DON'T THINK WE HAVE TO WORRY ABOUT THEM RAISING ANY ALARMS FOR A WHILE.
THAT SPELL PUNK WAS SO SCARED, I HOPE HE WAS TELLING THE TRUTH ABOUT OUR VEHICLES BEING IN THE HANGAR.
I'M SORRY, STORMBLADE, AM I PLAYING TOO ROUGH FOR YOU?
MAYBE NEXT TIME YOU CAN TRY HUGGING THE BAD GUYS UNTIL THEY SURRENDER!
CUT THE BICKERING, YOU TWO! WE GOT INTO THIS TOGETHER...
...AND THAT'S THE ONLY WAY OUT OF THIS. NONE OF US CAN DO THIS ON OUR OWN.
THE SOONER YOU FIGURE THAT OUT, THE SOONER YOU MIGHT BECOME ACTUAL SKYLANDERS!
YOU WANT TO BE HEROES? FINE. THEN START ACTING LIKE HEROES!
NOW LET'S FIND OUR VEHICLES AND GET OUT OF HERE.

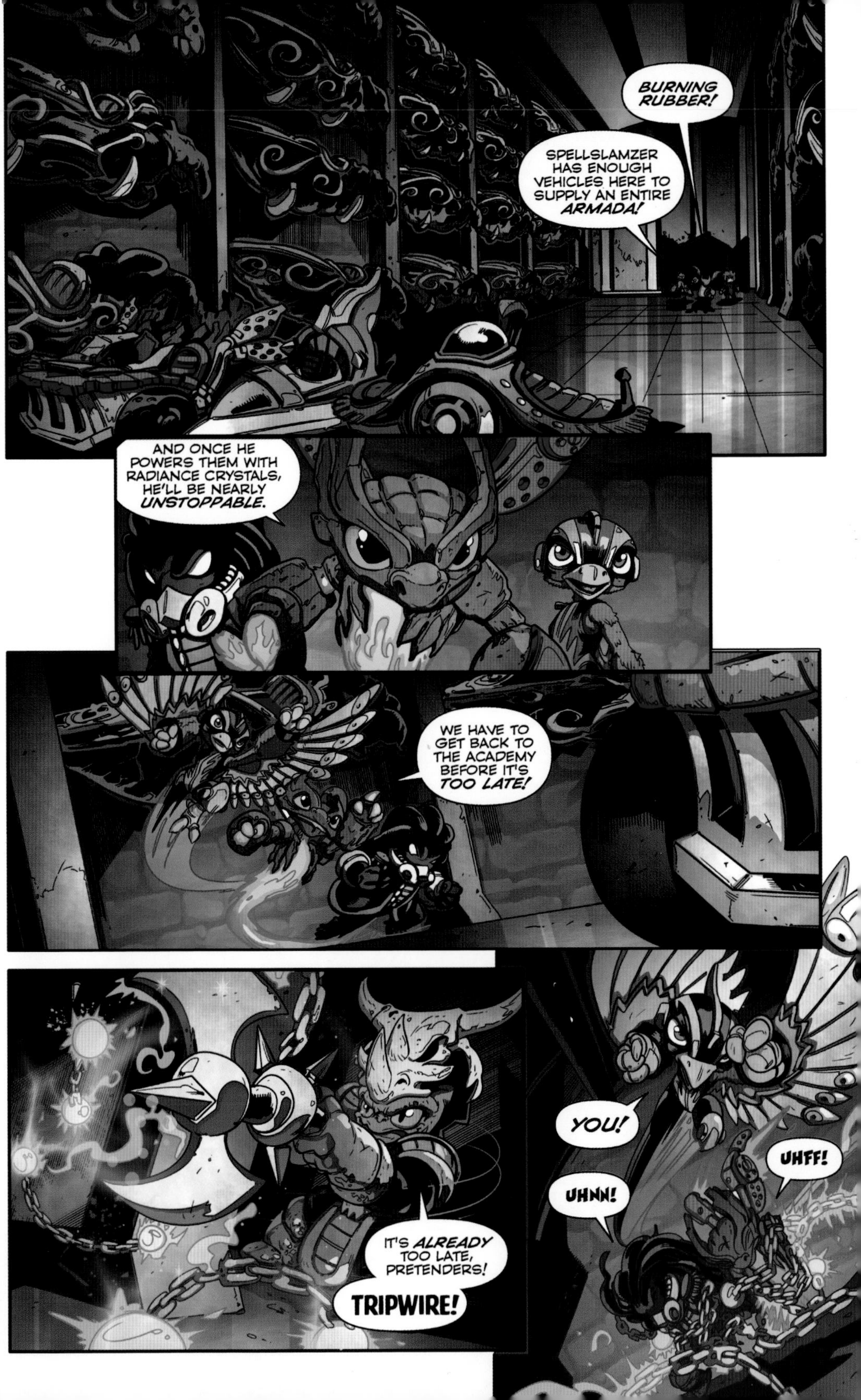
BURNING RUBBER!
SPELLSLAMZER HAS ENOUGH VEHICLES HERE TO SUPPLY AN ENTIRE ARMADA!
AND ONCE HE POWERS THEM WITH RADIANCE CRYSTALS, HE'LL BE NEARLY UNSTOPPABLE.
WE HAVE TO GET BACK TO THE ACADEMY BEFORE IT'S TOO LATE!
IT'S ALREADY TOO LATE, PRETENDERS!
TRIPWIRE!
YOU!
UHNN!
UHFF!

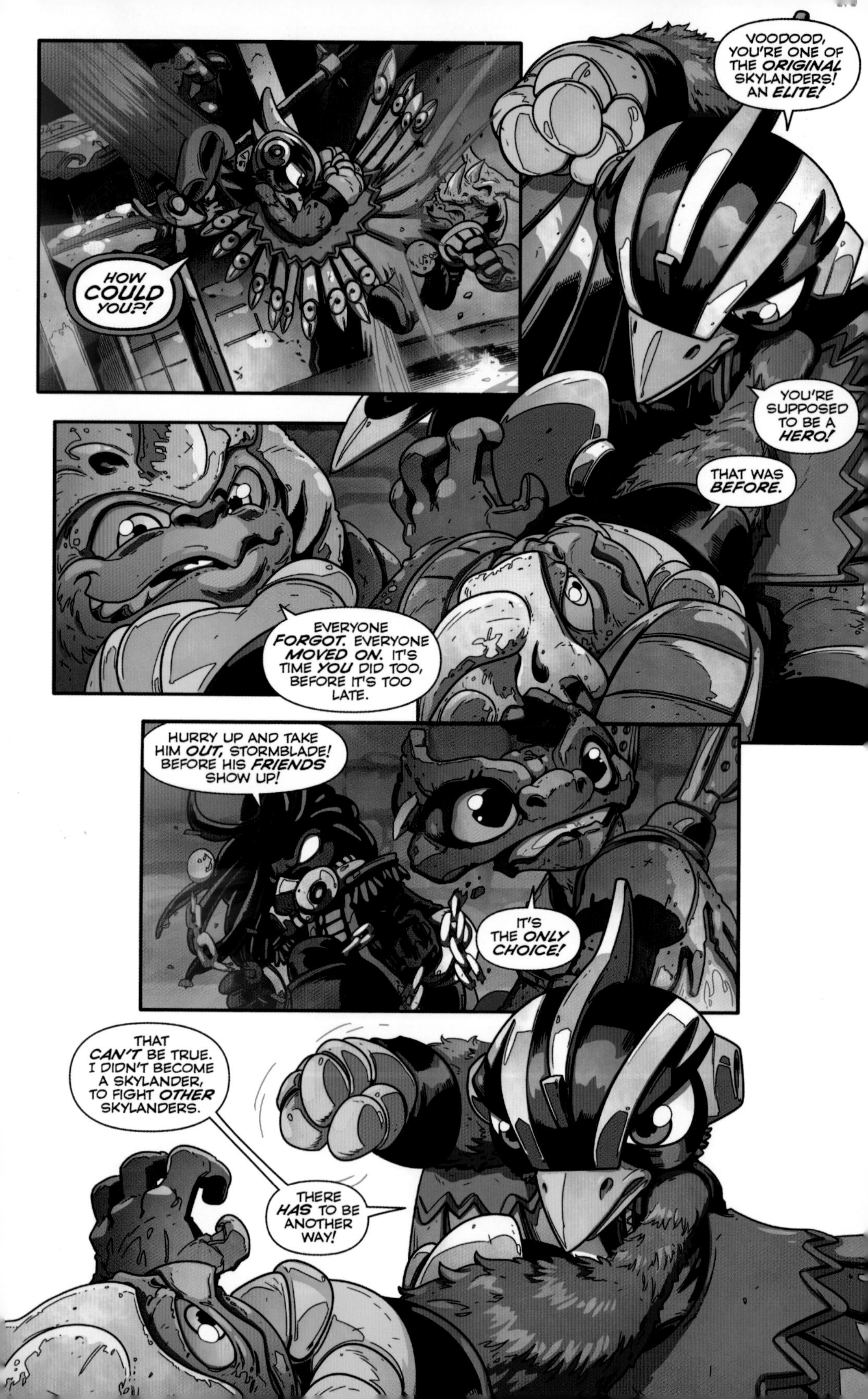
HOW COULD YOU?!
VOODOOD, YOU'RE ONE OF THE ORIGINAL SKYLANDERS! AN ELITE!
YOU'RE SUPPOSED TO BE A HERO!
THAT WAS BEFORE.
EVERYONE FORGOT. EVERYONE MOVED ON. IT'S TIME YOU DID TOO, BEFORE IT'S TOO LATE.
HURRY UP AND TAKE HIM OUT, STORMBLADE! BEFORE HIS FRIENDS SHOW UP!
IT'S THE ONLY CHOICE!
THAT CAN'T BE TRUE. I DIDN'T BECOME A SKYLANDER, TO FIGHT OTHER SKYLANDERS.
THERE HAS TO BE ANOTHER WAY!

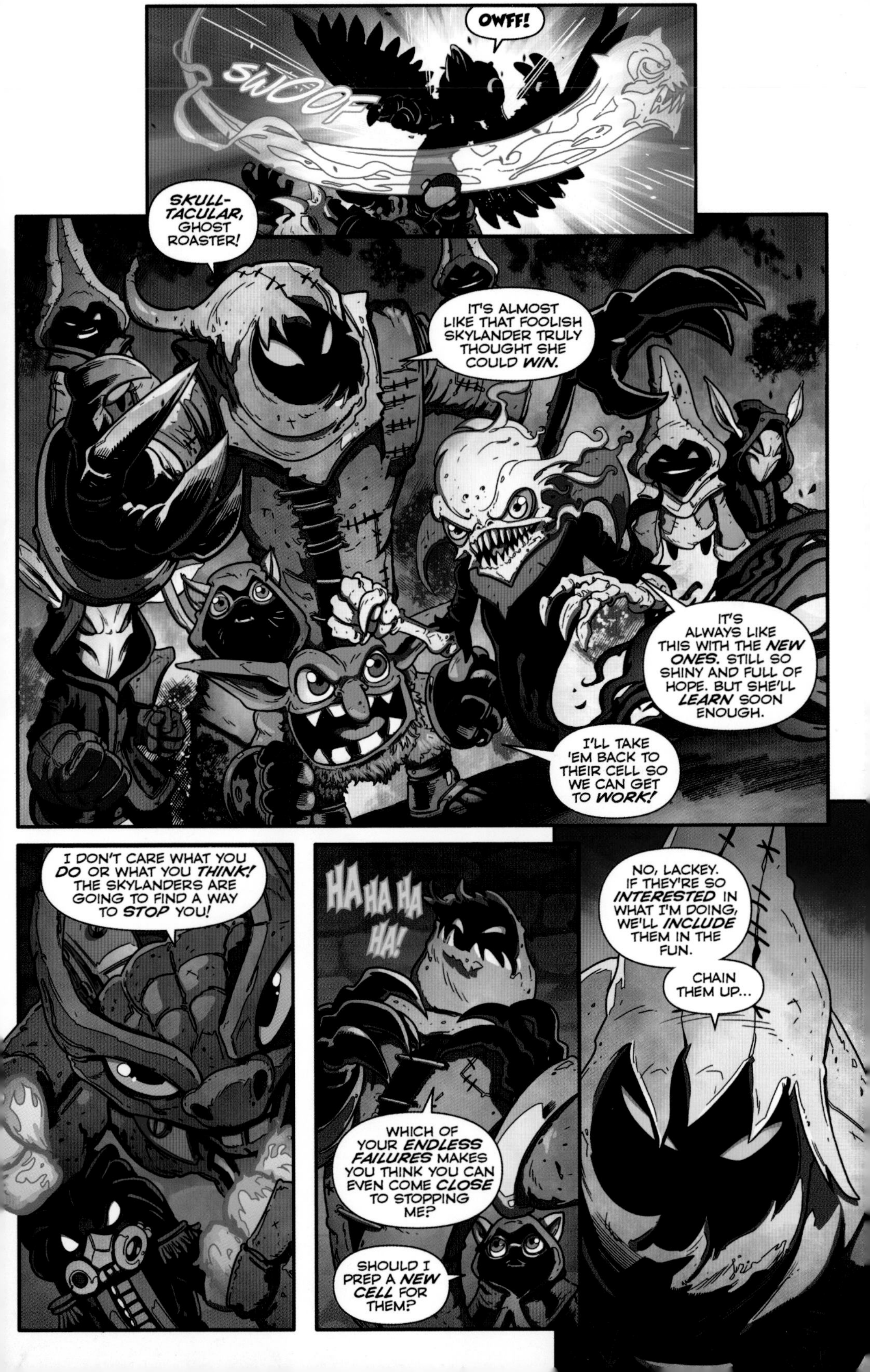
OWFF!
SWOOF
SKULL-TACULAR, GHOST ROASTER!
IT'S ALMOST LIKE THAT FOOLISH SKYLANDER TRULY THOUGHT SHE COULD WIN.
IT'S ALWAYS LIKE THIS WITH THE NEW ONES. STILL SO SHINY AND FULL OF HOPE. BUT SHE'LL LEARN SOON ENOUGH.
I'LL TAKE 'EM BACK TO THEIR CELL SO WE CAN GET TO WORK!
I DON'T CARE WHAT YOU DO OR WHAT YOU THINK! THE SKYLANDERS ARE GOING TO FIND A WAY TO STOP YOU!
HA HA HA HA!
WHICH OF YOUR ENDLESS FAILURES MAKES YOU THINK YOU CAN EVEN COME CLOSE TO STOPPING ME?
SHOULD I PREP A NEW CELL FOR THEM?
NO, LACKEY. IF THEY'RE SO INTERESTED IN WHAT I'M DOING, WE'LL INCLUDE THEM IN THE FUN.
CHAIN THEM UP...

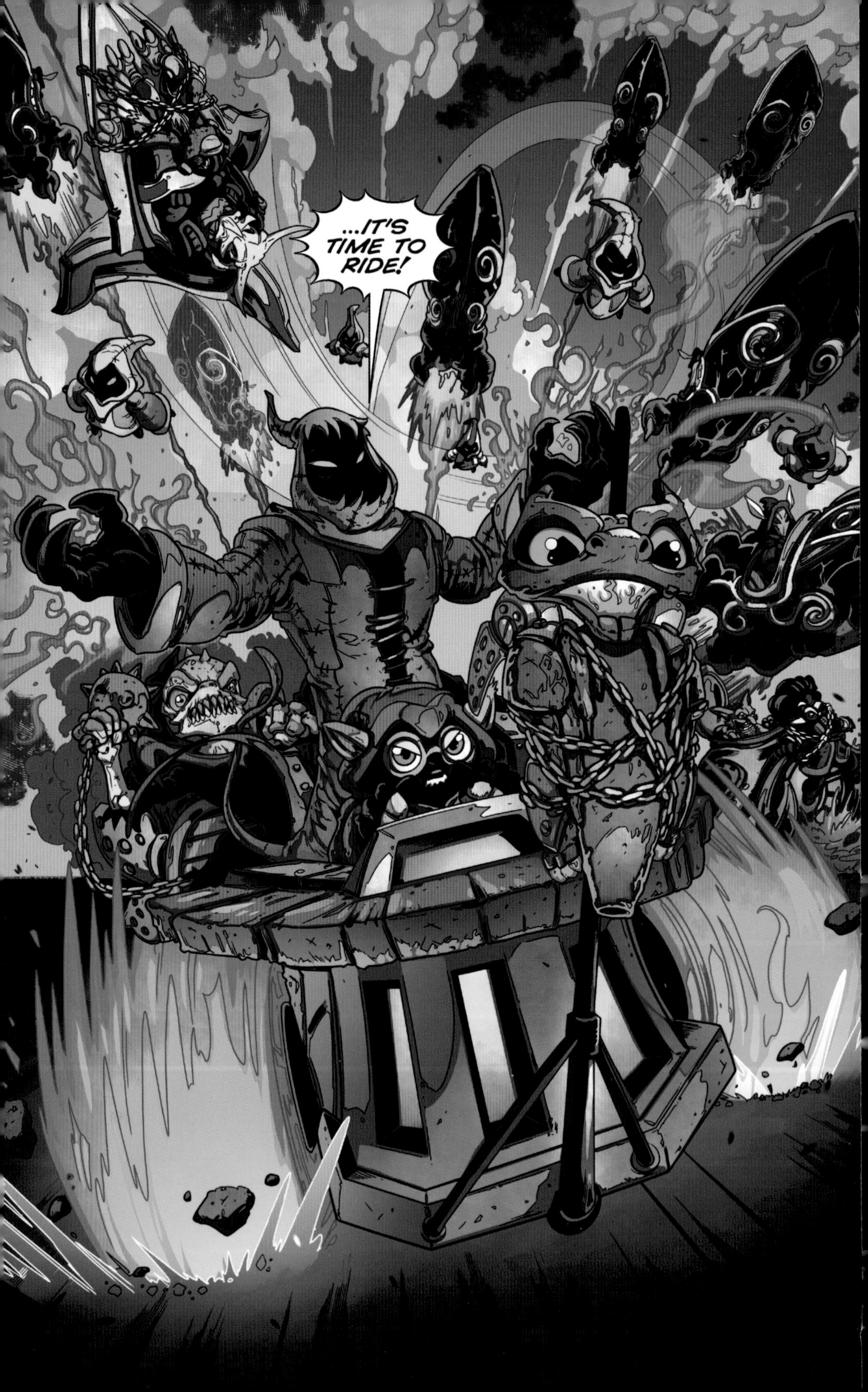
...IT'S TIME TO RIDE!

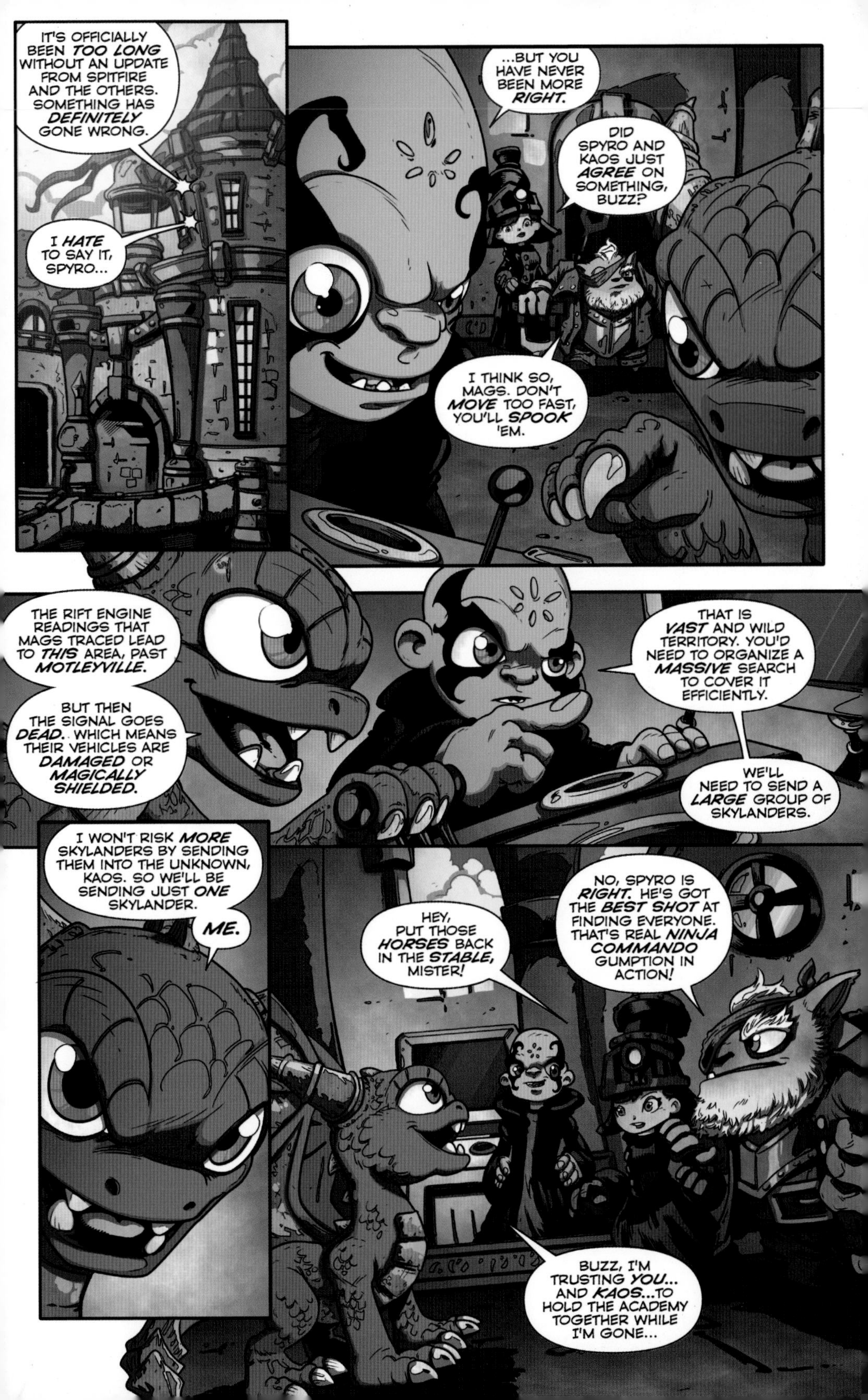
IT'S OFFICIALLY BEEN TOO LONG WITHOUT AN UPDATE FROM SPITFIRE AND THE OTHERS. SOMETHING HAS DEFINITELY GONE WRONG.
I HATE TO SAY IT, SPYRO...
...BUT YOU HAVE NEVER BEEN MORE RIGHT.
DID SPYRO AND KAOS JUST AGREE ON SOMETHING, BUZZ?
I THINK SO, MAGS. DON'T MOVE TOO FAST, YOU'LL SPOOK 'EM.
THE RIFT ENGINE READINGS THAT MAGS TRACED LEAD TO THIS AREA, PAST MOTLEYVILLE.
BUT THEN THE SIGNAL GOES DEAD. WHICH MEANS THEIR VEHICLES ARE DAMAGED OR MAGICALLY SHIELDED.
THAT IS VAST AND WILD TERRITORY. YOU'D NEED TO ORGANIZE A MASSIVE SEARCH TO COVER IT EFFICIENTLY.
WE'LL NEED TO SEND A LARGE GROUP OF SKYLANDERS.
I WON'T RISK MORE SKYLANDERS BY SENDING THEM INTO THE UNKNOWN, KAOS. SO WE'LL BE SENDING JUST ONE SKYLANDER.
ME.
HEY, PUT THOSE HORSES BACK IN THE STABLE, MISTER!
NO, SPYRO IS RIGHT. HE'S GOT THE BEST SHOT AT FINDING EVERYONE. THAT'S REAL NINJA COMMANDO GUMPTION IN ACTION!
BUZZ, I'M TRUSTING YOU... AND KAOS...TO HOLD THE ACADEMY TOGETHER WHILE I'M GONE...

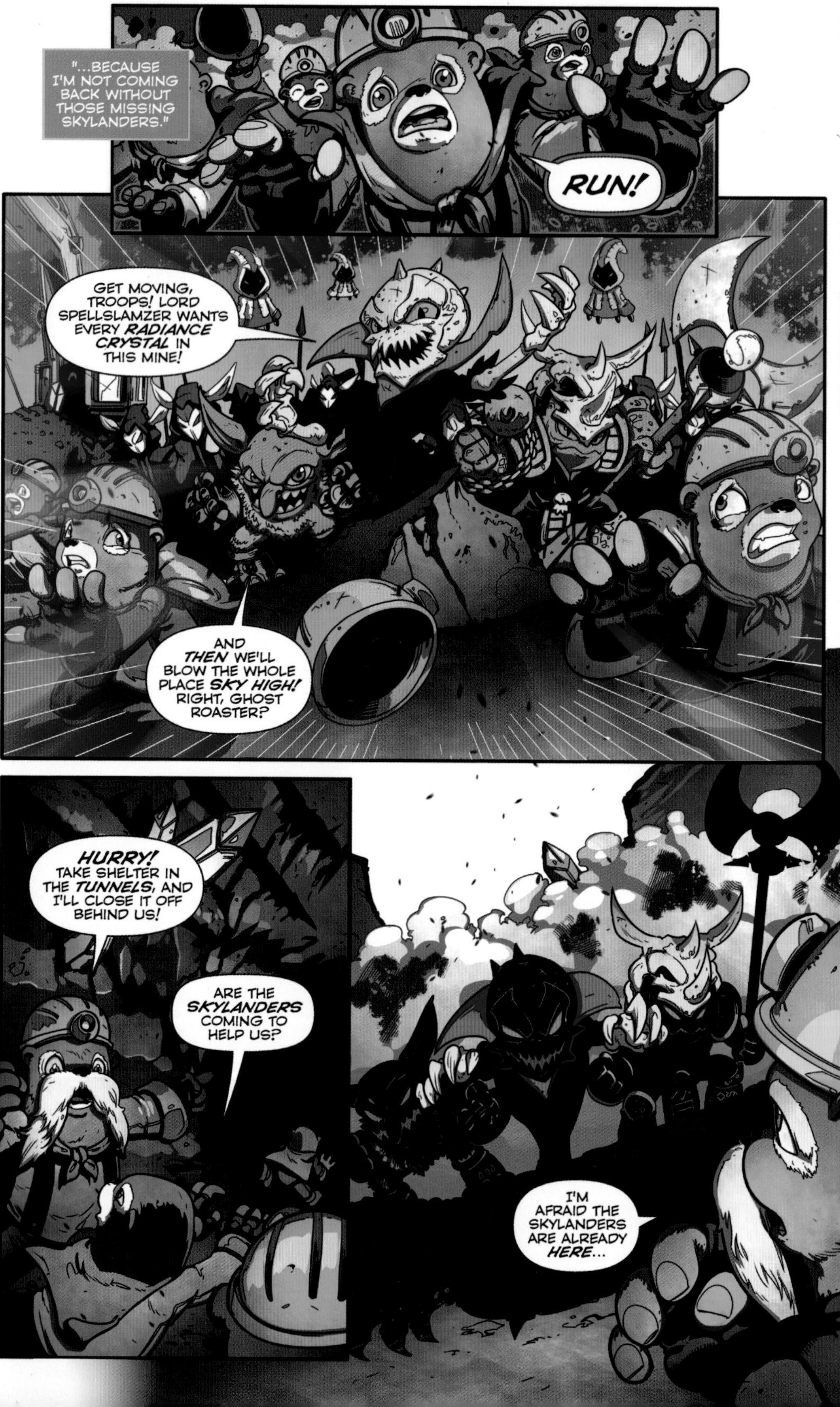
"...BECAUSE I'M NOT COMING BACK WITHOUT THOSE MISSING SKYLANDERS."
RUN!
GET MOVING, TROOPS! LORD SPELLSLAMZER WANTS EVERY *RADIANCE CRYSTAL* IN THIS MINE!
AND *THEN* WE'LL BLOW THE WHOLE PLACE *SKY HIGH!* RIGHT, GHOST ROASTER?
HURRY! TAKE SHELTER IN THE *TUNNELS*, AND I'LL CLOSE IT OFF BEHIND US!
ARE THE *SKYLANDERS* COMING TO HELP US?
I'M AFRAID THE SKYLANDERS ARE ALREADY *HERE*...

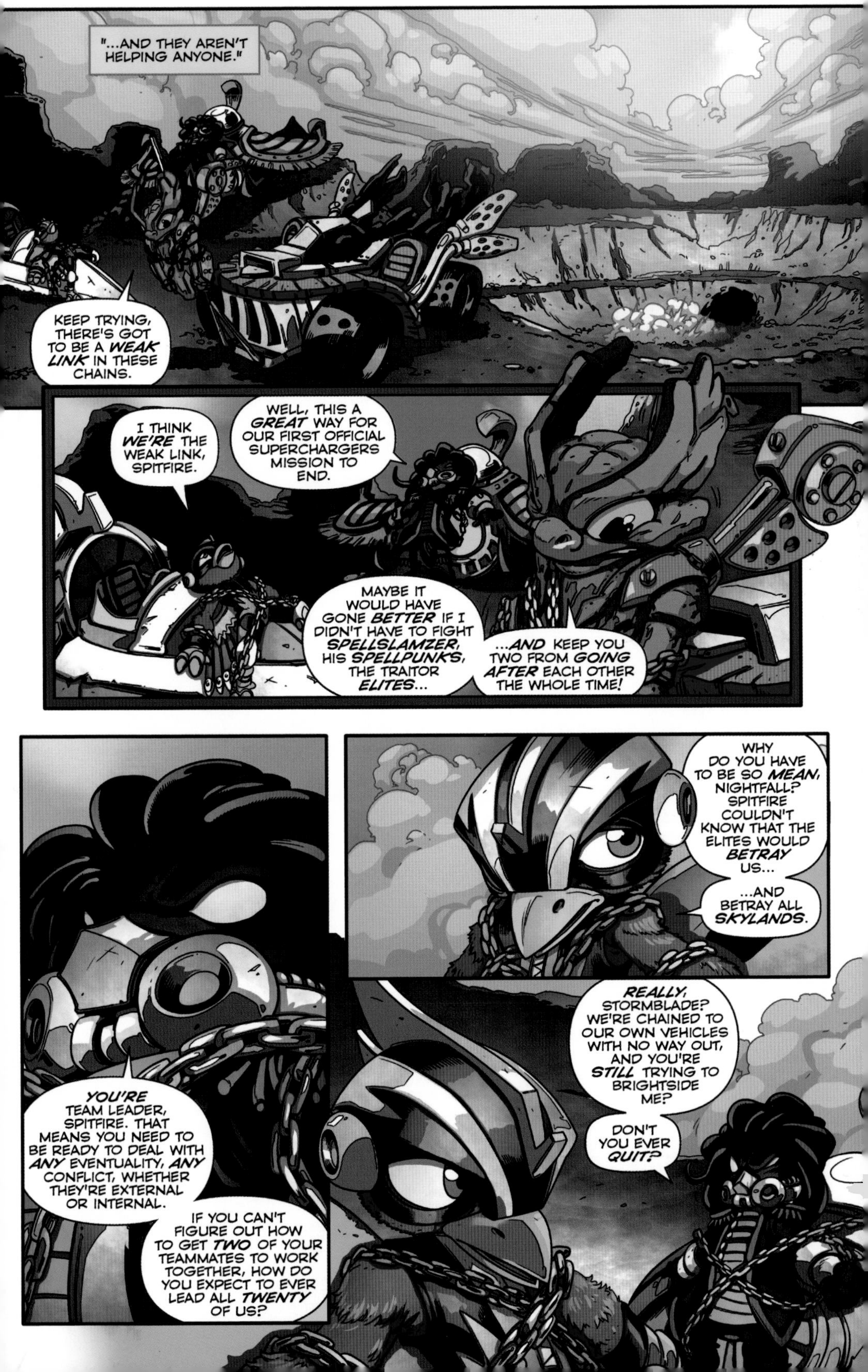
"...AND THEY AREN'T HELPING ANYONE."
KEEP TRYING, THERE'S GOT TO BE A WEAK LINK IN THESE CHAINS.
I THINK WE'RE THE WEAK LINK, SPITFIRE.
WELL, THIS A GREAT WAY FOR OUR FIRST OFFICIAL SUPERCHARGERS MISSION TO END.
MAYBE IT WOULD HAVE GONE BETTER IF I DIDN'T HAVE TO FIGHT SPELLSLAMZER, HIS SPELLPUNKS, THE TRAITOR ELITES...
...AND KEEP YOU TWO FROM GOING AFTER EACH OTHER THE WHOLE TIME!
YOU'RE TEAM LEADER, SPITFIRE. THAT MEANS YOU NEED TO BE READY TO DEAL WITH ANY EVENTUALITY, ANY CONFLICT, WHETHER THEY'RE EXTERNAL OR INTERNAL.
IF YOU CAN'T FIGURE OUT HOW TO GET TWO OF YOUR TEAMMATES TO WORK TOGETHER, HOW DO YOU EXPECT TO EVER LEAD ALL TWENTY OF US?
WHY DO YOU HAVE TO BE SO MEAN, NIGHTFALL? SPITFIRE COULDN'T KNOW THAT THE ELITES WOULD BETRAY US...
...AND BETRAY ALL SKYLANDS.
REALLY, STORMBLADE? WE'RE CHAINED TO OUR OWN VEHICLES WITH NO WAY OUT, AND YOU'RE STILL TRYING TO BRIGHTSIDE ME?
DON'T YOU EVER QUIT?

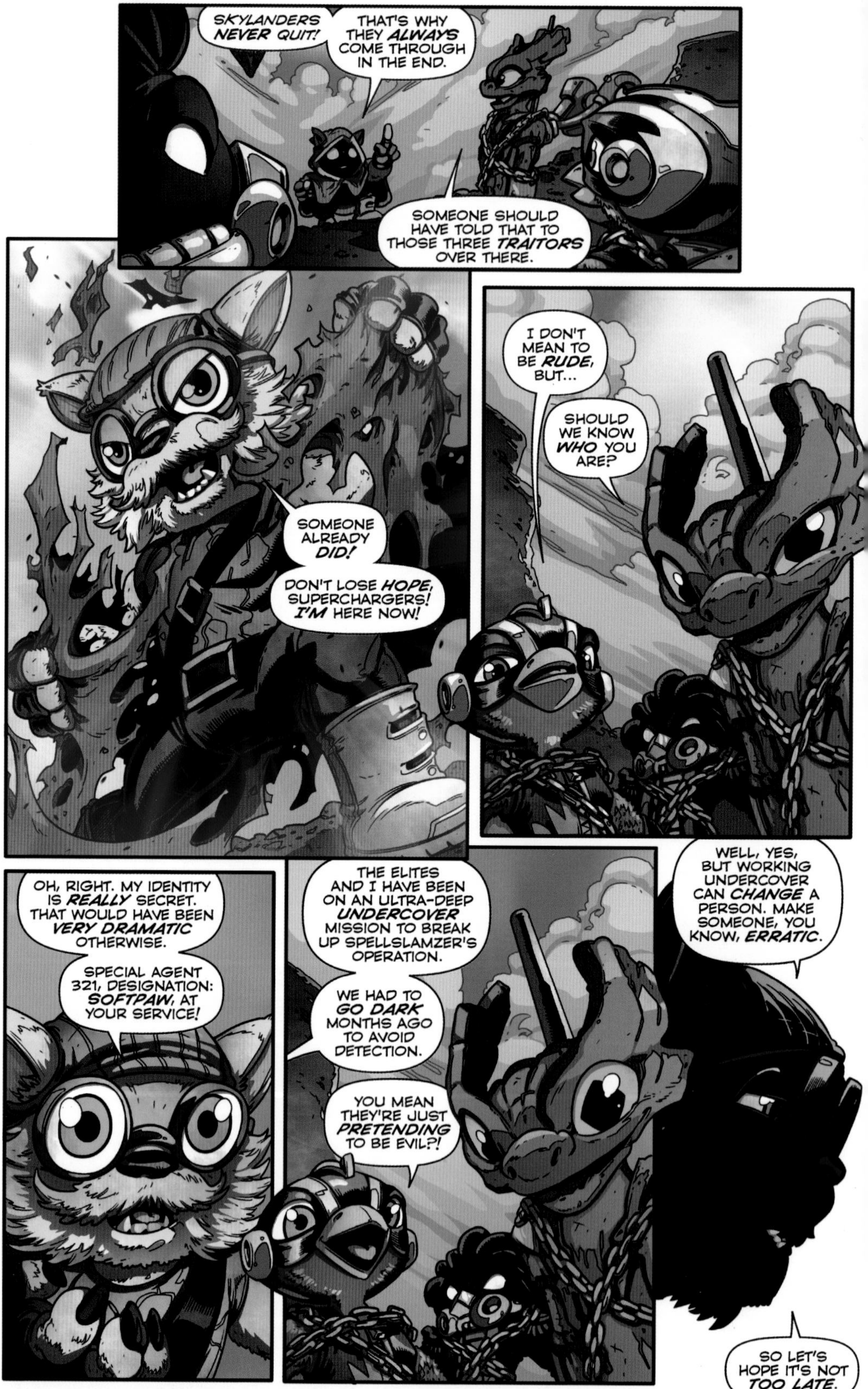
SKYLANDERS NEVER QUIT!
THAT'S WHY THEY ALWAYS COME THROUGH IN THE END.
SOMEONE SHOULD HAVE TOLD THAT TO THOSE THREE TRAITORS OVER THERE.
SOMEONE ALREADY DID!
DON'T LOSE HOPE, SUPERCHARGERS! I'M HERE NOW!
I DON'T MEAN TO BE RUDE, BUT...
SHOULD WE KNOW WHO YOU ARE?
OH, RIGHT. MY IDENTITY IS REALLY SECRET. THAT WOULD HAVE BEEN VERY DRAMATIC OTHERWISE.
SPECIAL AGENT 321, DESIGNATION: SOFTPAW, AT YOUR SERVICE!
THE ELITES AND I HAVE BEEN ON AN ULTRA-DEEP UNDERCOVER MISSION TO BREAK UP SPELLSLAMZER'S OPERATION.
WE HAD TO GO DARK MONTHS AGO TO AVOID DETECTION.
YOU MEAN THEY'RE JUST PRETENDING TO BE EVIL?!
WELL, YES, BUT WORKING UNDERCOVER CAN CHANGE A PERSON. MAKE SOMEONE, YOU KNOW, ERRATIC.
SO LET'S HOPE IT'S NOT TOO LATE.

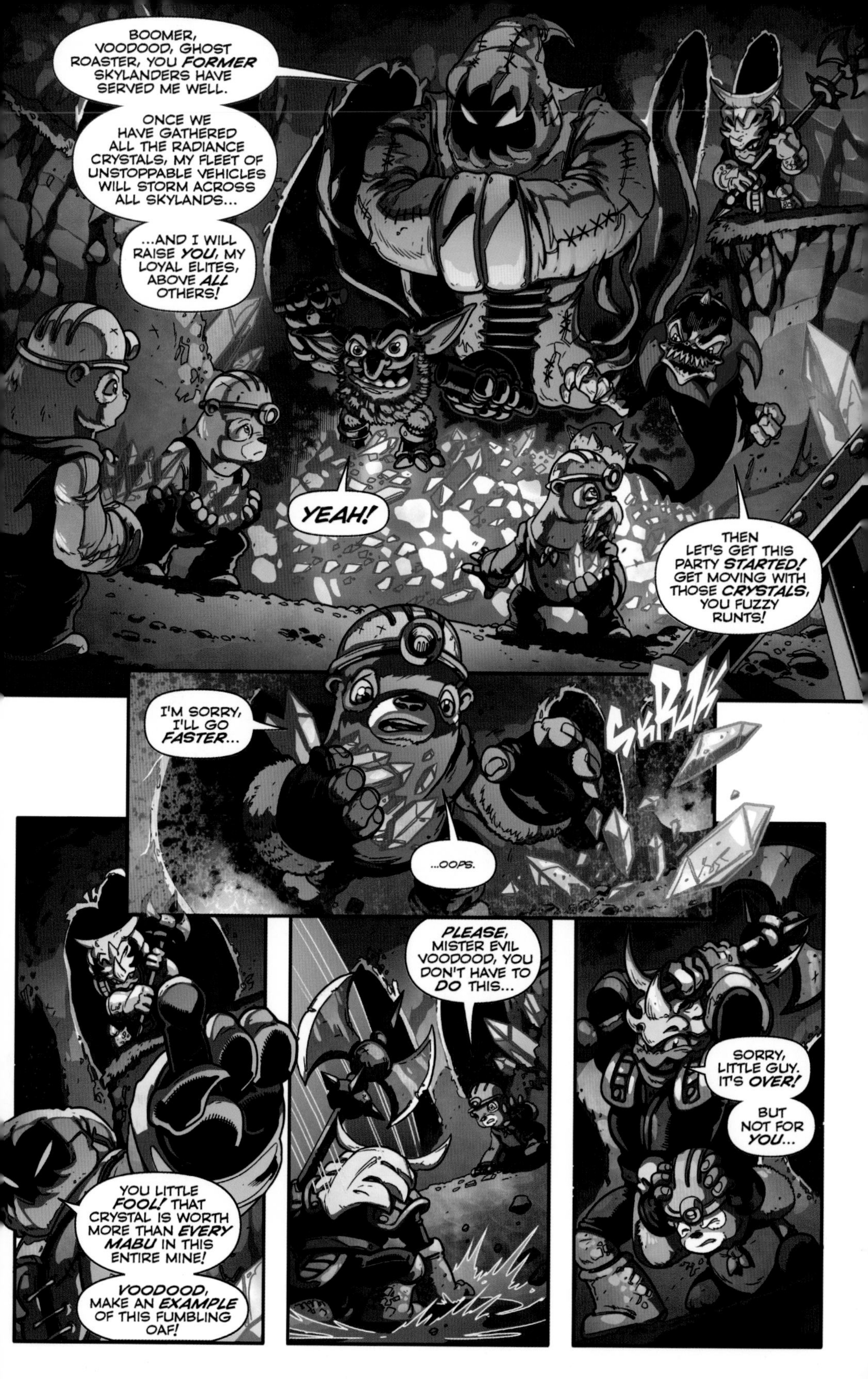
BOOMER, VOODOOD, GHOST ROASTER, YOU FORMER SKYLANDERS HAVE SERVED ME WELL.
ONCE WE HAVE GATHERED ALL THE RADIANCE CRYSTALS, MY FLEET OF UNSTOPPABLE VEHICLES WILL STORM ACROSS ALL SKYLANDS...
...AND I WILL RAISE YOU, MY LOYAL ELITES, ABOVE ALL OTHERS!
YEAH!
THEN LET'S GET THIS PARTY STARTED! GET MOVING WITH THOSE CRYSTALS, YOU FUZZY RUNTS!
I'M SORRY, I'LL GO FASTER...
SKRAK
...OOPS.
YOU LITTLE FOOL! THAT CRYSTAL IS WORTH MORE THAN EVERY MABU IN THIS ENTIRE MINE!
VOODOOD, MAKE AN EXAMPLE OF THIS FUMBLING OAF!
PLEASE, MISTER EVIL VOODOOD, YOU DON'T HAVE TO DO THIS...
SORRY, LITTLE GUY. IT'S OVER!
BUT NOT FOR YOU...

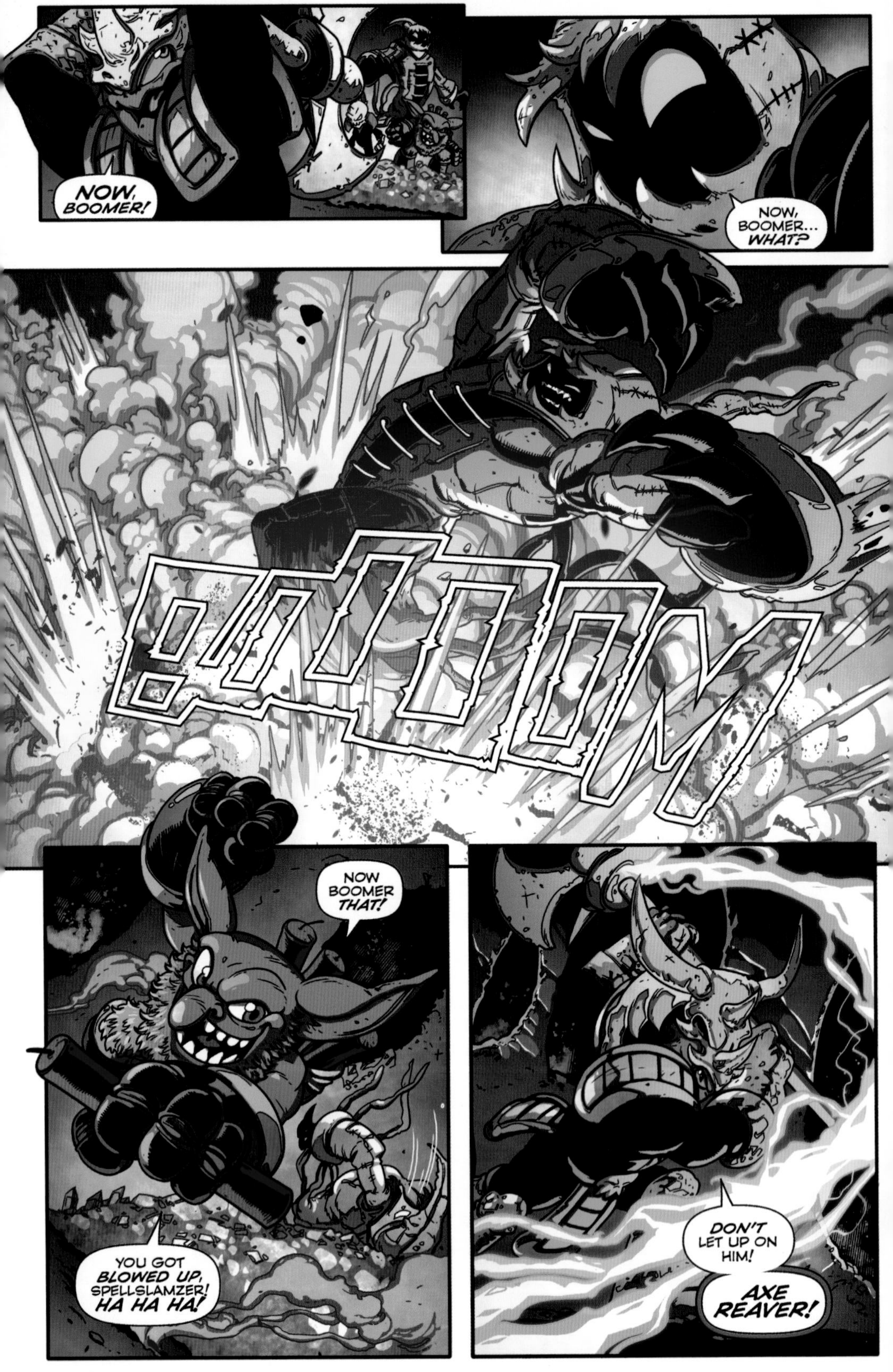
NOW, BOOMER!
NOW, BOOMER... WHAT?
KA-BOOM
NOW BOOMER THAT!
YOU GOT BLOWED UP, SPELLSLAMZER! HA HA HA!
DON'T LET UP ON HIM!
AXE REAVER!

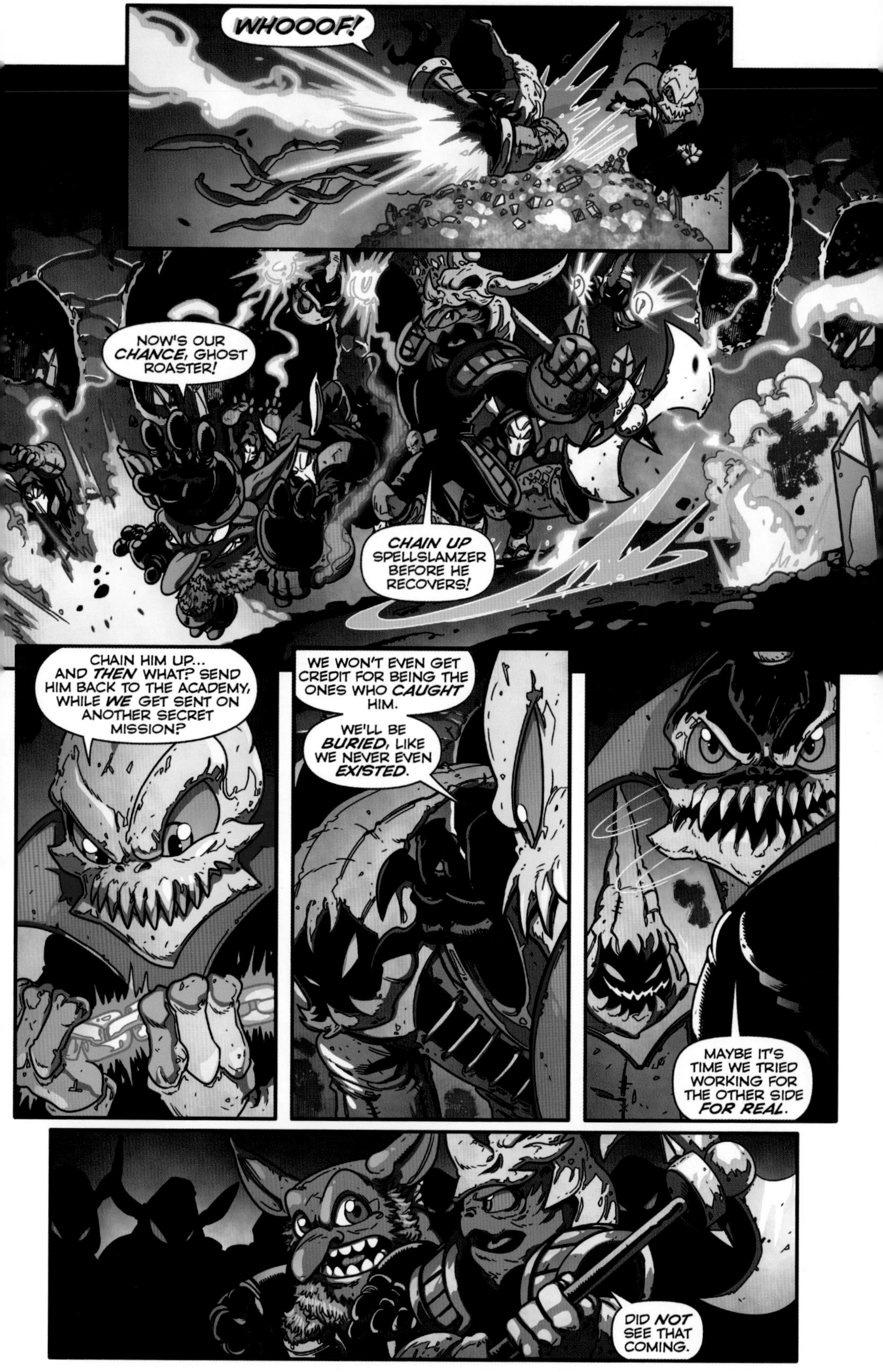
WHOOOF!
NOW'S OUR CHANCE, GHOST ROASTER!
CHAIN UP SPELLSLAMZER BEFORE HE RECOVERS!
CHAIN HIM UP... AND THEN WHAT? SEND HIM BACK TO THE ACADEMY, WHILE WE GET SENT ON ANOTHER SECRET MISSION?
WE WON'T EVEN GET CREDIT FOR BEING THE ONES WHO CAUGHT HIM.
WE'LL BE BURIED, LIKE WE NEVER EVEN EXISTED.
MAYBE IT'S TIME WE TRIED WORKING FOR THE OTHER SIDE FOR REAL.
DID NOT SEE THAT COMING.

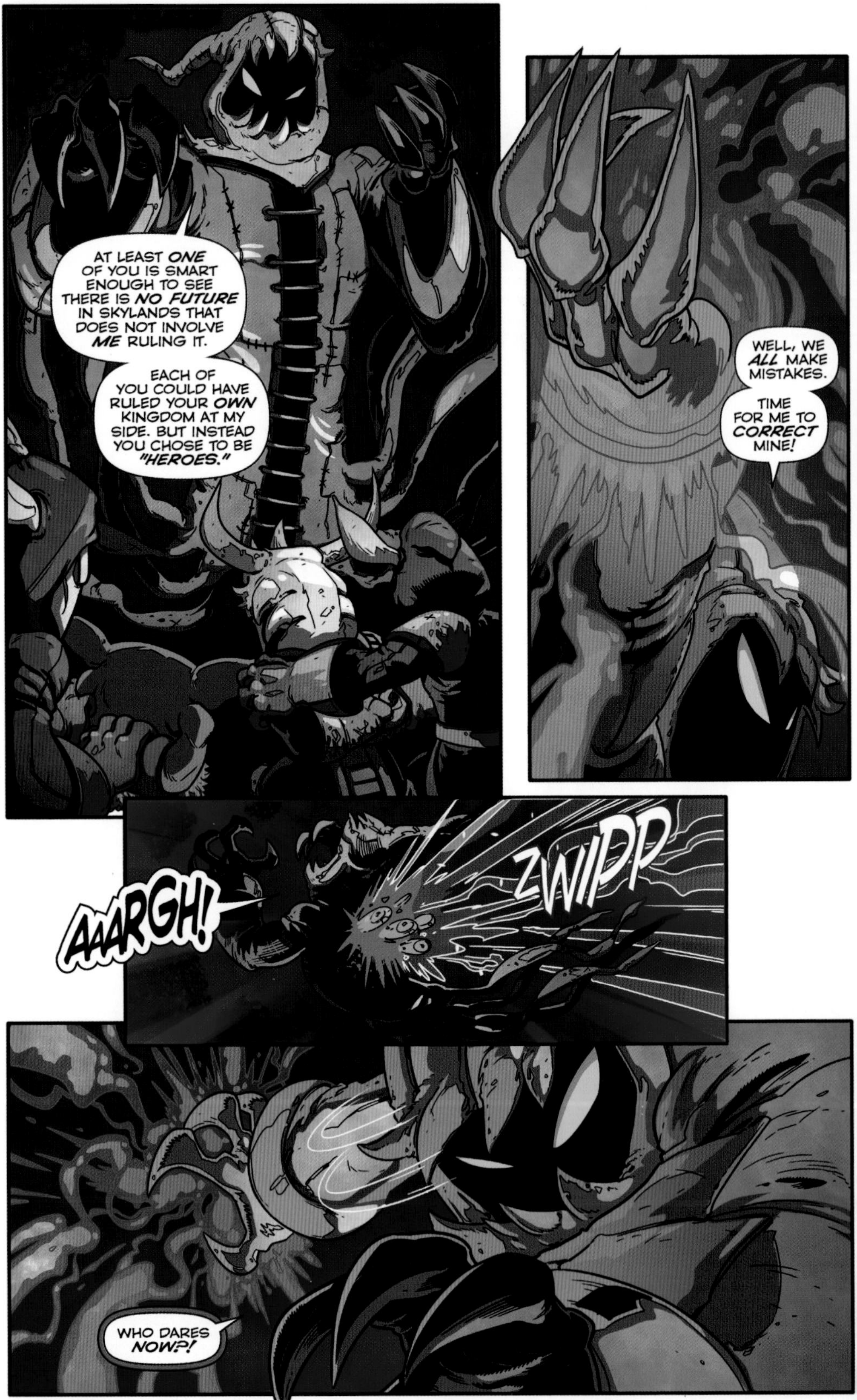
AT LEAST ONE OF YOU IS SMART ENOUGH TO SEE THERE IS NO FUTURE IN SKYLANDS THAT DOES NOT INVOLVE ME RULING IT.
EACH OF YOU COULD HAVE RULED YOUR OWN KINGDOM AT MY SIDE. BUT INSTEAD YOU CHOSE TO BE "HEROES."
WELL, WE ALL MAKE MISTAKES.
TIME FOR ME TO CORRECT MINE!
ZWIPP
AAARGH!
WHO DARES NOW?!

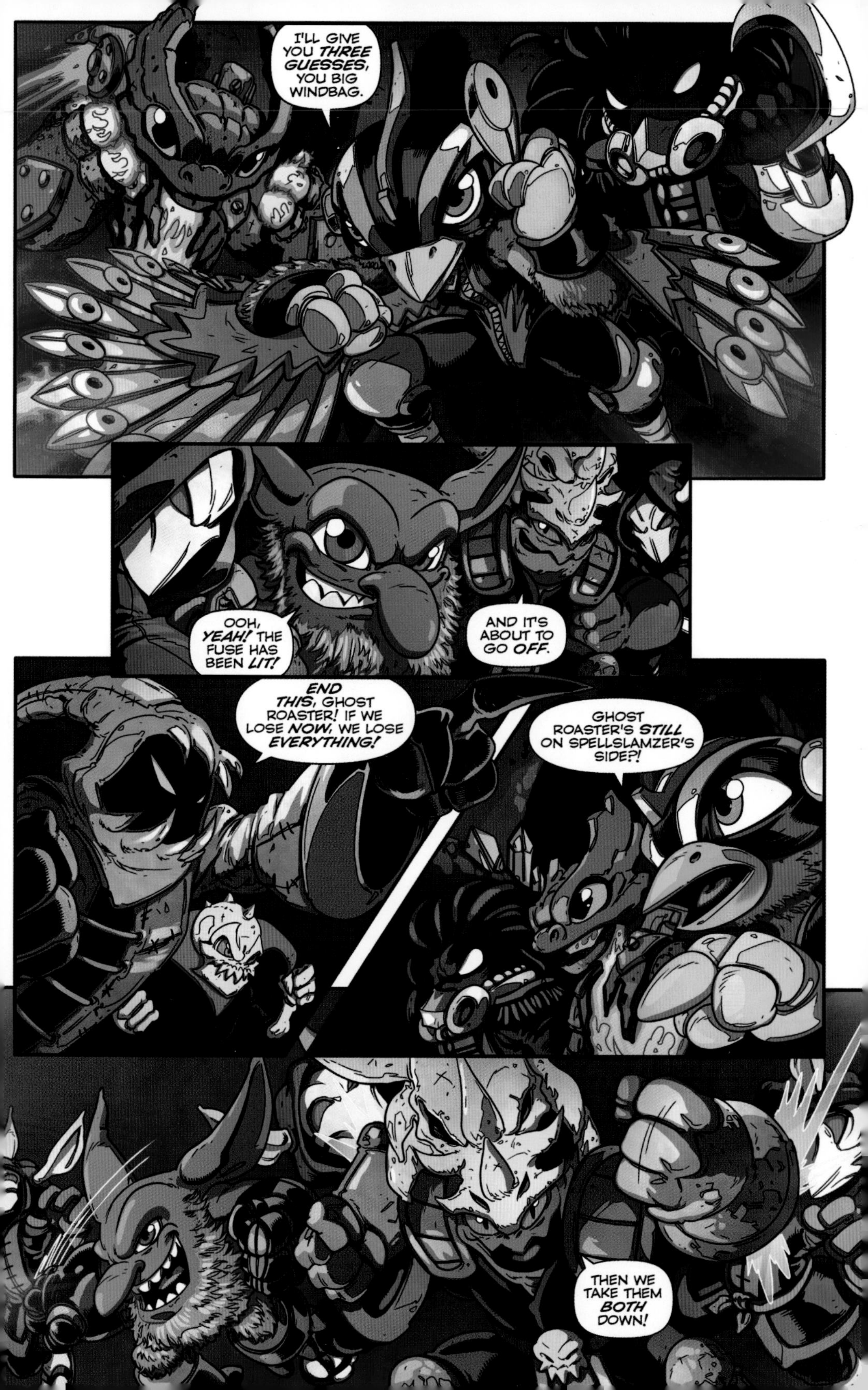
I'LL GIVE YOU *THREE GUESSES*, YOU BIG WINDBAG.
OOH, *YEAH!* THE FUSE HAS BEEN *LIT!*
AND IT'S ABOUT TO GO *OFF*.
END THIS, GHOST ROASTER! IF WE LOSE *NOW*, WE LOSE *EVERYTHING!*
GHOST ROASTER'S *STILL* ON SPELLSLAMZER'S SIDE?!
THEN WE TAKE THEM *BOTH* DOWN!

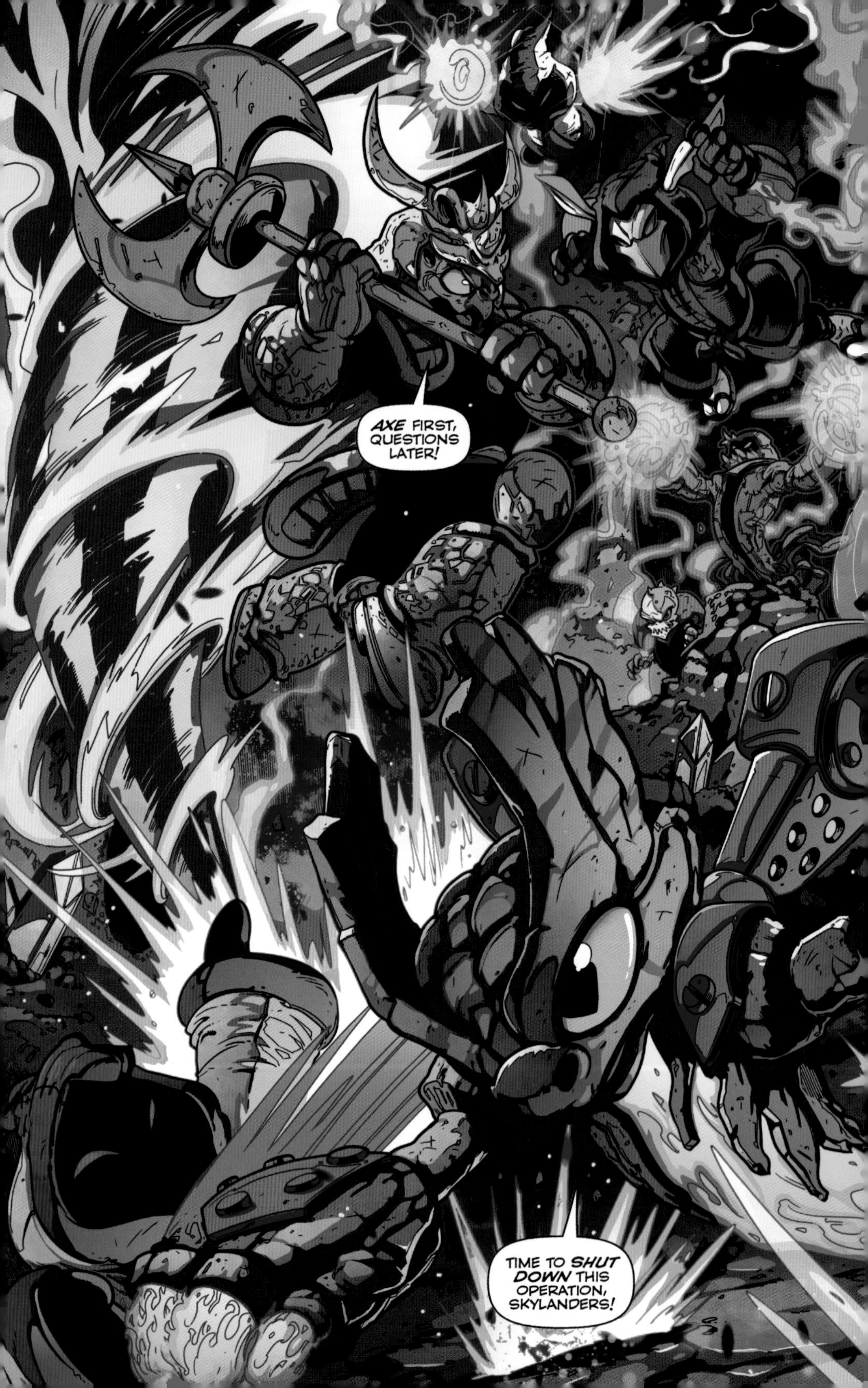
AXE FIRST, QUESTIONS LATER!
TIME TO SHUT DOWN THIS OPERATION, SKYLANDERS!

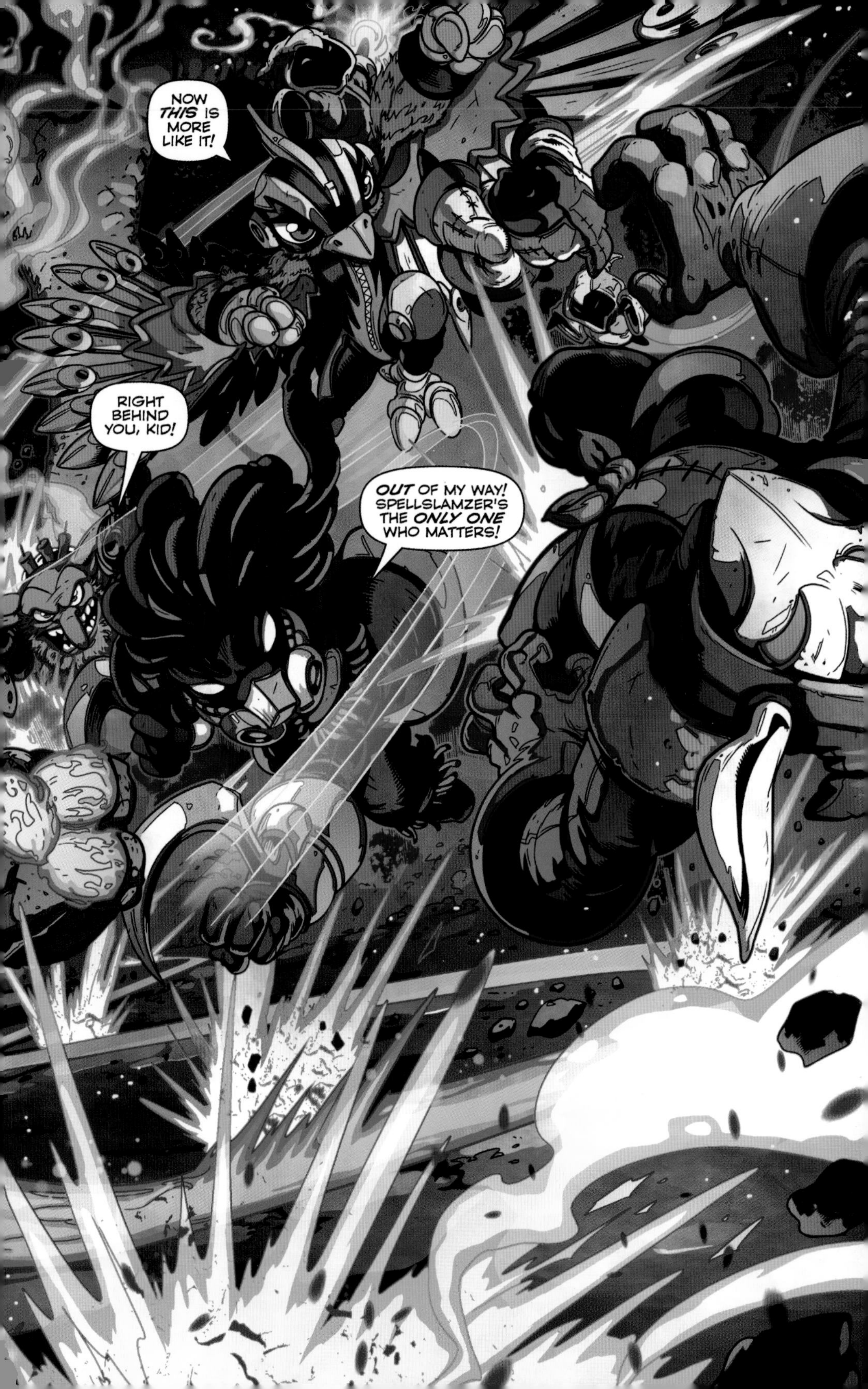
NOW *THIS* IS MORE LIKE IT!
RIGHT BEHIND YOU, KID!
OUT OF MY WAY! SPELLSLAMZER'S THE *ONLY ONE* WHO MATTERS!

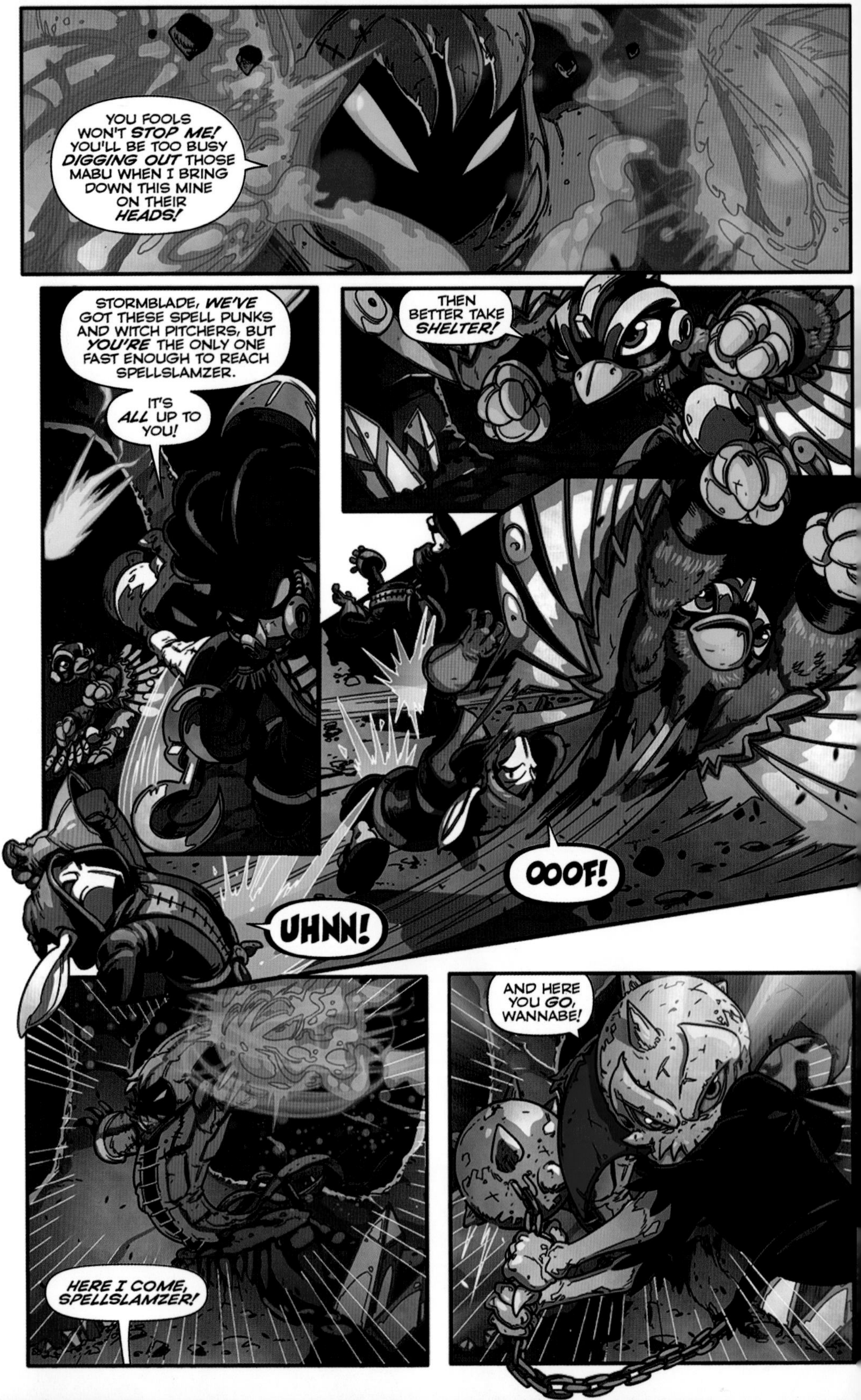
YOU FOOLS WON'T STOP ME! YOU'LL BE TOO BUSY DIGGING OUT THOSE MABU WHEN I BRING DOWN THIS MINE ON THEIR HEADS!
STORMBLADE, WE'VE GOT THESE SPELL PUNKS AND WITCH PITCHERS, BUT YOU'RE THE ONLY ONE FAST ENOUGH TO REACH SPELLSLAMZER.
IT'S ALL UP TO YOU!
THEN BETTER TAKE SHELTER!
OOOF!
UHNN!
HERE I COME, SPELLSLAMZER!
AND HERE YOU GO, WANNABE!

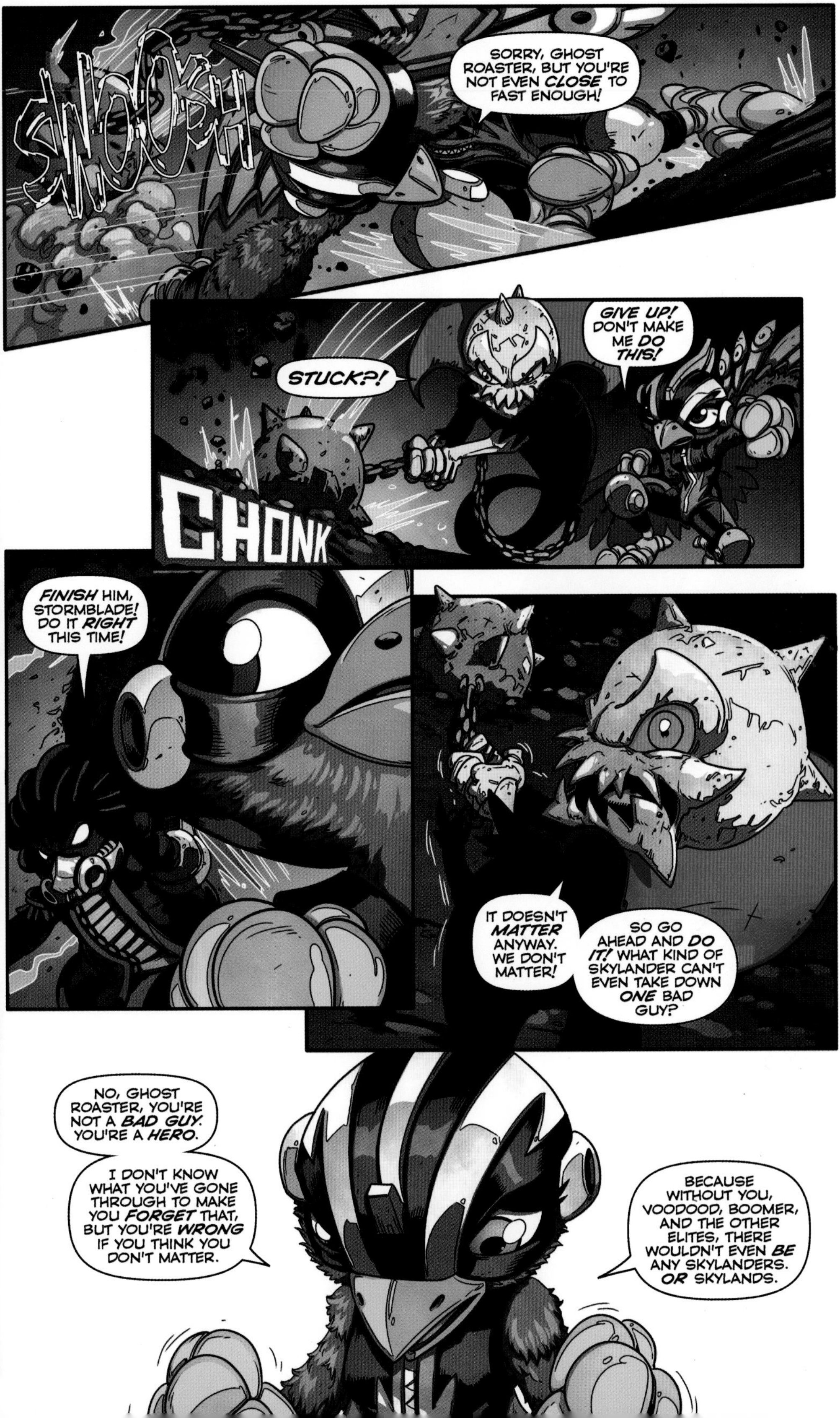
SWOOOSH
SORRY, GHOST ROASTER, BUT YOU'RE NOT EVEN CLOSE TO FAST ENOUGH!
STUCK?!
GIVE UP! DON'T MAKE ME DO THIS!
CHONK
FINISH HIM, STORMBLADE! DO IT RIGHT THIS TIME!
IT DOESN'T MATTER ANYWAY. WE DON'T MATTER!
SO GO AHEAD AND DO IT! WHAT KIND OF SKYLANDER CAN'T EVEN TAKE DOWN ONE BAD GUY?
NO, GHOST ROASTER, YOU'RE NOT A BAD GUY. YOU'RE A HERO.
I DON'T KNOW WHAT YOU'VE GONE THROUGH TO MAKE YOU FORGET THAT, BUT YOU'RE WRONG IF YOU THINK YOU DON'T MATTER.
BECAUSE WITHOUT YOU, VOODOOD, BOOMER, AND THE OTHER ELITES, THERE WOULDN'T EVEN BE ANY SKYLANDERS. OR SKYLANDS.

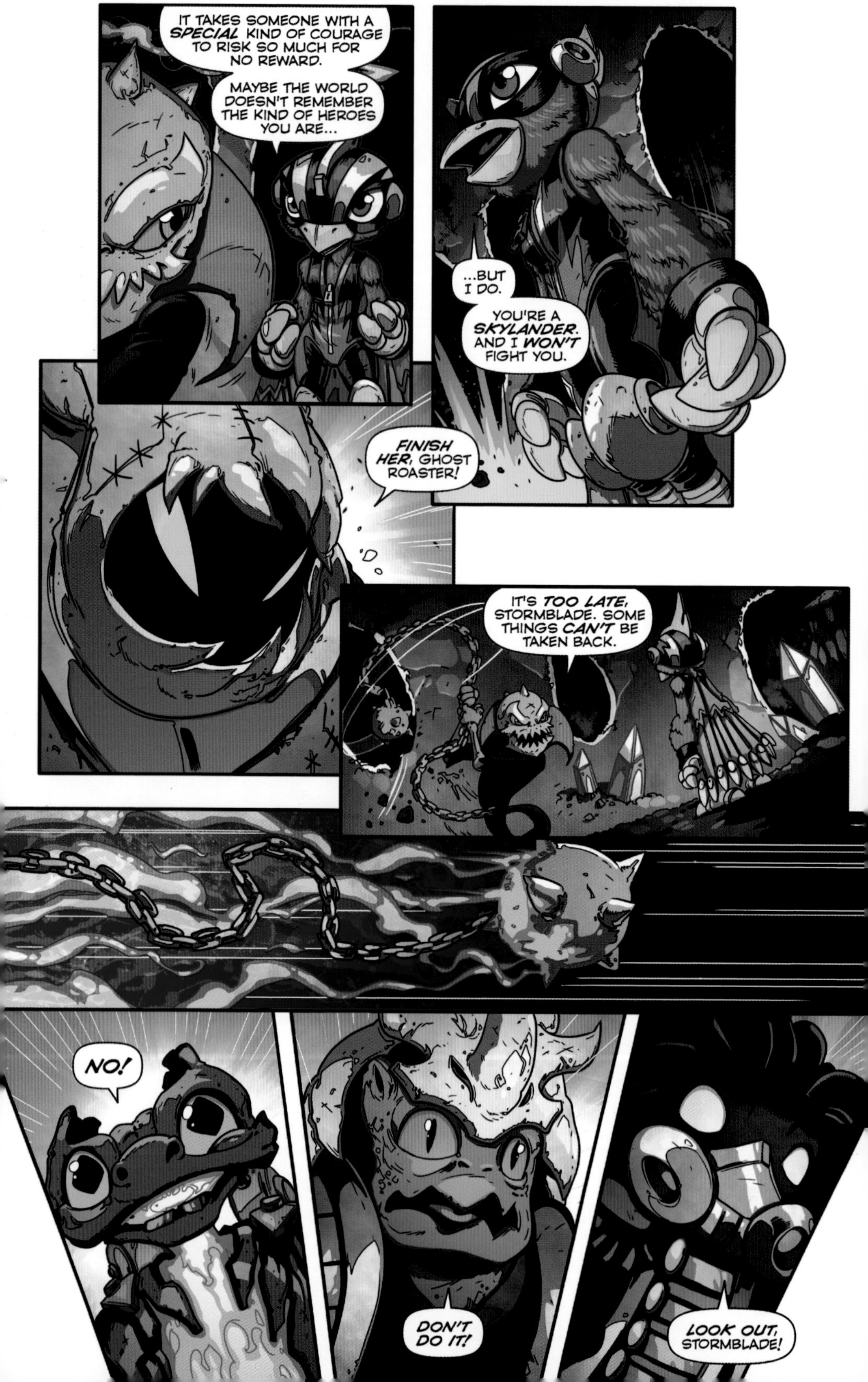
IT TAKES SOMEONE WITH A SPECIAL KIND OF COURAGE TO RISK SO MUCH FOR NO REWARD.
MAYBE THE WORLD DOESN'T REMEMBER THE KIND OF HEROES YOU ARE...
...BUT I DO.
YOU'RE A SKYLANDER. AND I WON'T FIGHT YOU.
FINISH HER, GHOST ROASTER!
IT'S TOO LATE, STORMBLADE. SOME THINGS CAN'T BE TAKEN BACK.
NO!
DON'T DO IT!
LOOK OUT, STORMBLADE!

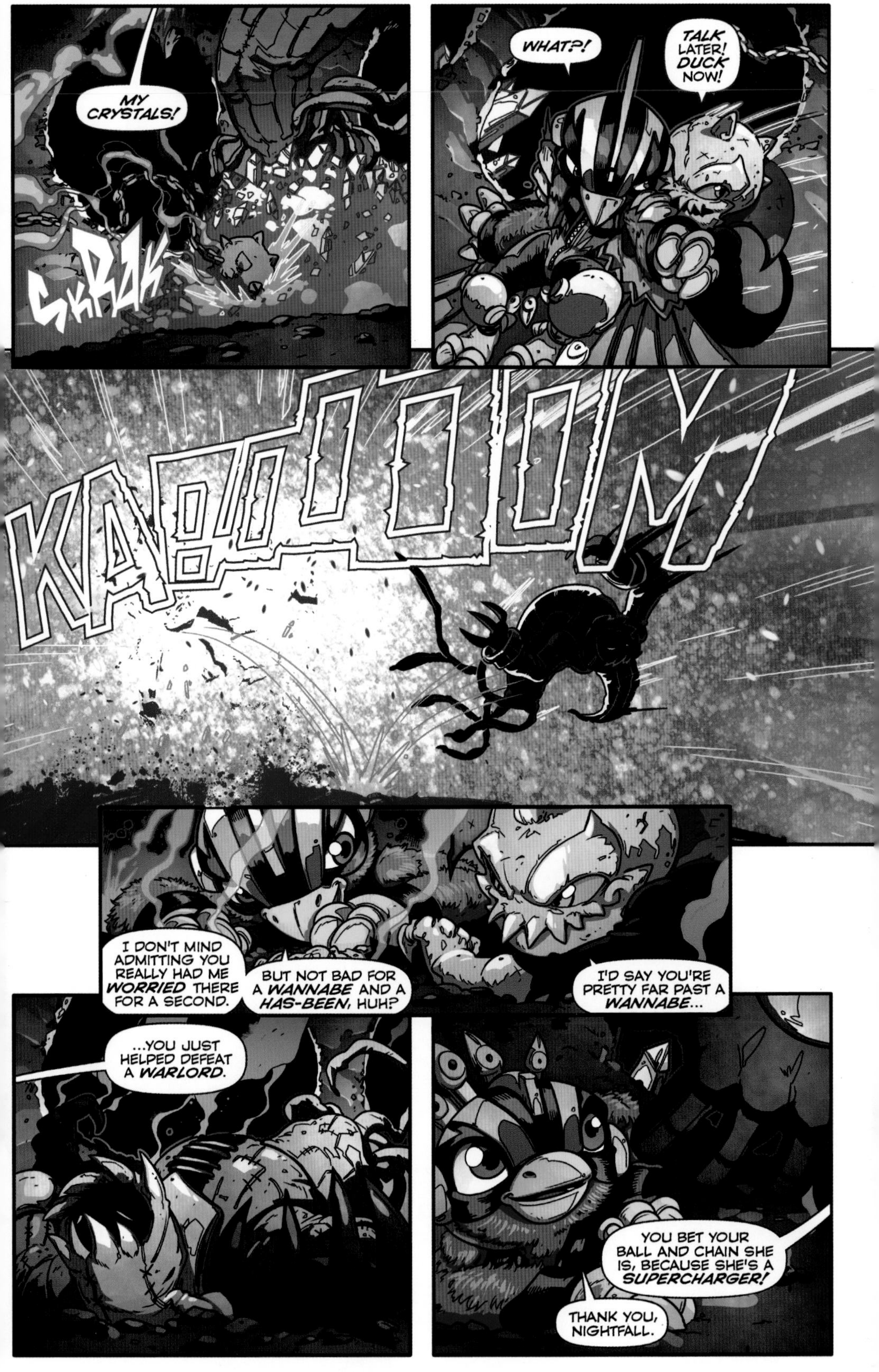
MY CRYSTALS!
SKRAK
WHAT?!
TALK LATER! DUCK NOW!
KABOOOOOM
I DON'T MIND ADMITTING YOU REALLY HAD ME WORRIED THERE FOR A SECOND.
BUT NOT BAD FOR A WANNABE AND A HAS-BEEN, HUH?
I'D SAY YOU'RE PRETTY FAR PAST A WANNABE...
...YOU JUST HELPED DEFEAT A WARLORD.
YOU BET YOUR BALL AND CHAIN SHE IS, BECAUSE SHE'S A SUPERCHARGER!
THANK YOU, NIGHTFALL.

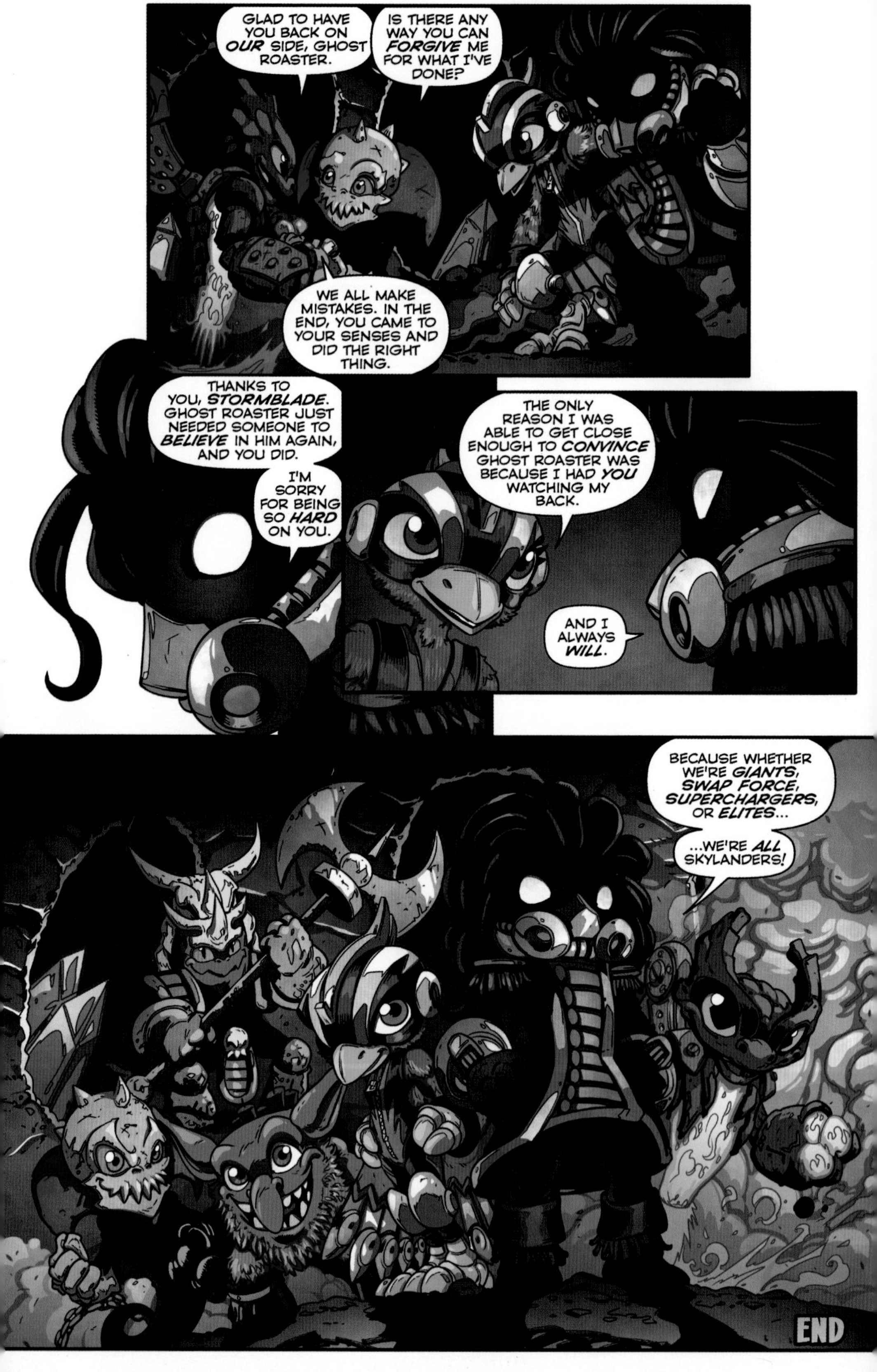
GLAD TO HAVE YOU BACK ON OUR SIDE, GHOST ROASTER.
IS THERE ANY WAY YOU CAN FORGIVE ME FOR WHAT I'VE DONE?
WE ALL MAKE MISTAKES. IN THE END, YOU CAME TO YOUR SENSES AND DID THE RIGHT THING.
THANKS TO YOU, STORMBLADE. GHOST ROASTER JUST NEEDED SOMEONE TO BELIEVE IN HIM AGAIN, AND YOU DID.
I'M SORRY FOR BEING SO HARD ON YOU.
THE ONLY REASON I WAS ABLE TO GET CLOSE ENOUGH TO CONVINCE GHOST ROASTER WAS BECAUSE I HAD YOU WATCHING MY BACK.
AND I ALWAYS WILL.
BECAUSE WHETHER WE'RE GIANTS, SWAP FORCE, SUPERCHARGERS, OR ELITES...
...WE'RE ALL SKYLANDERS!
END

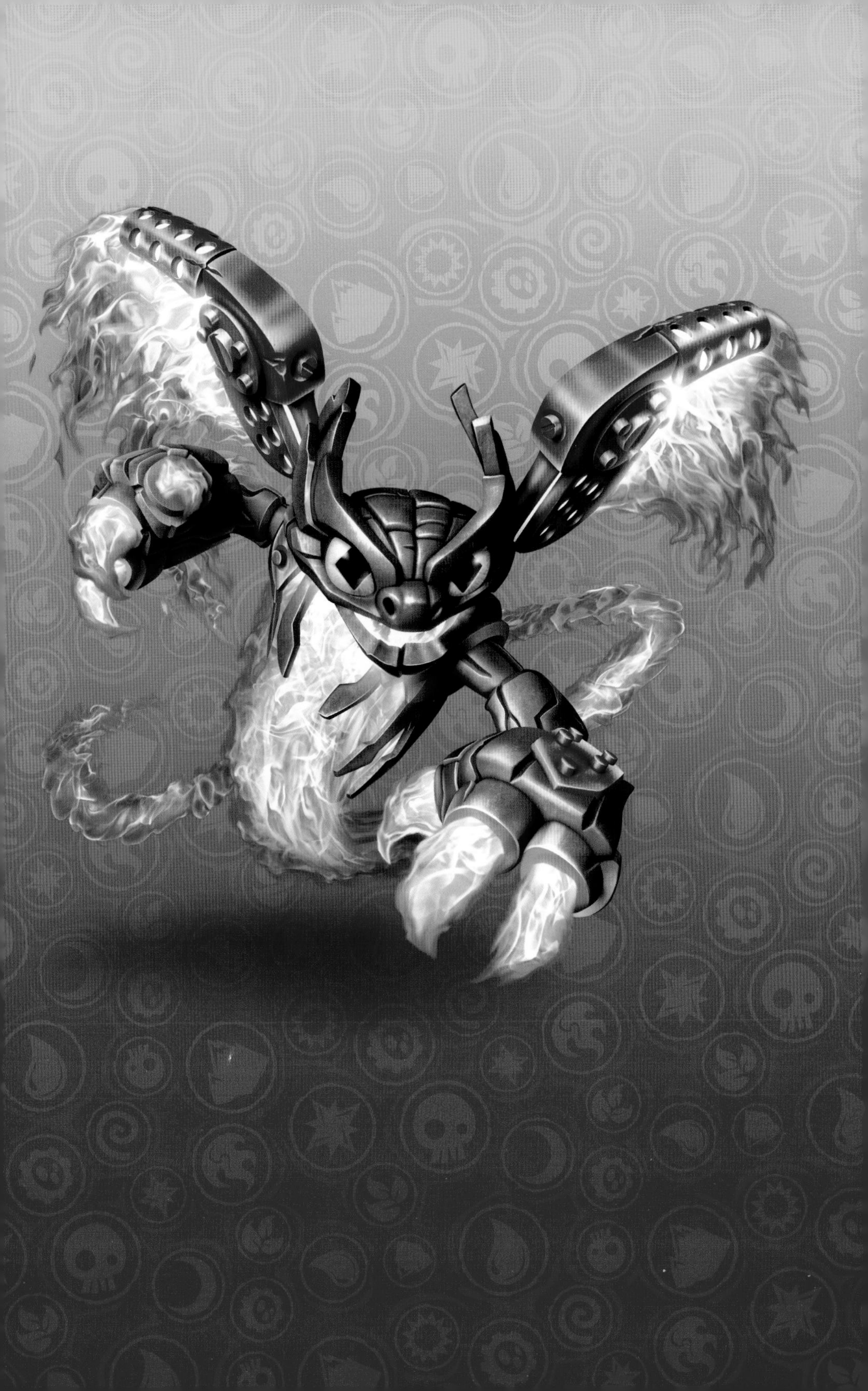

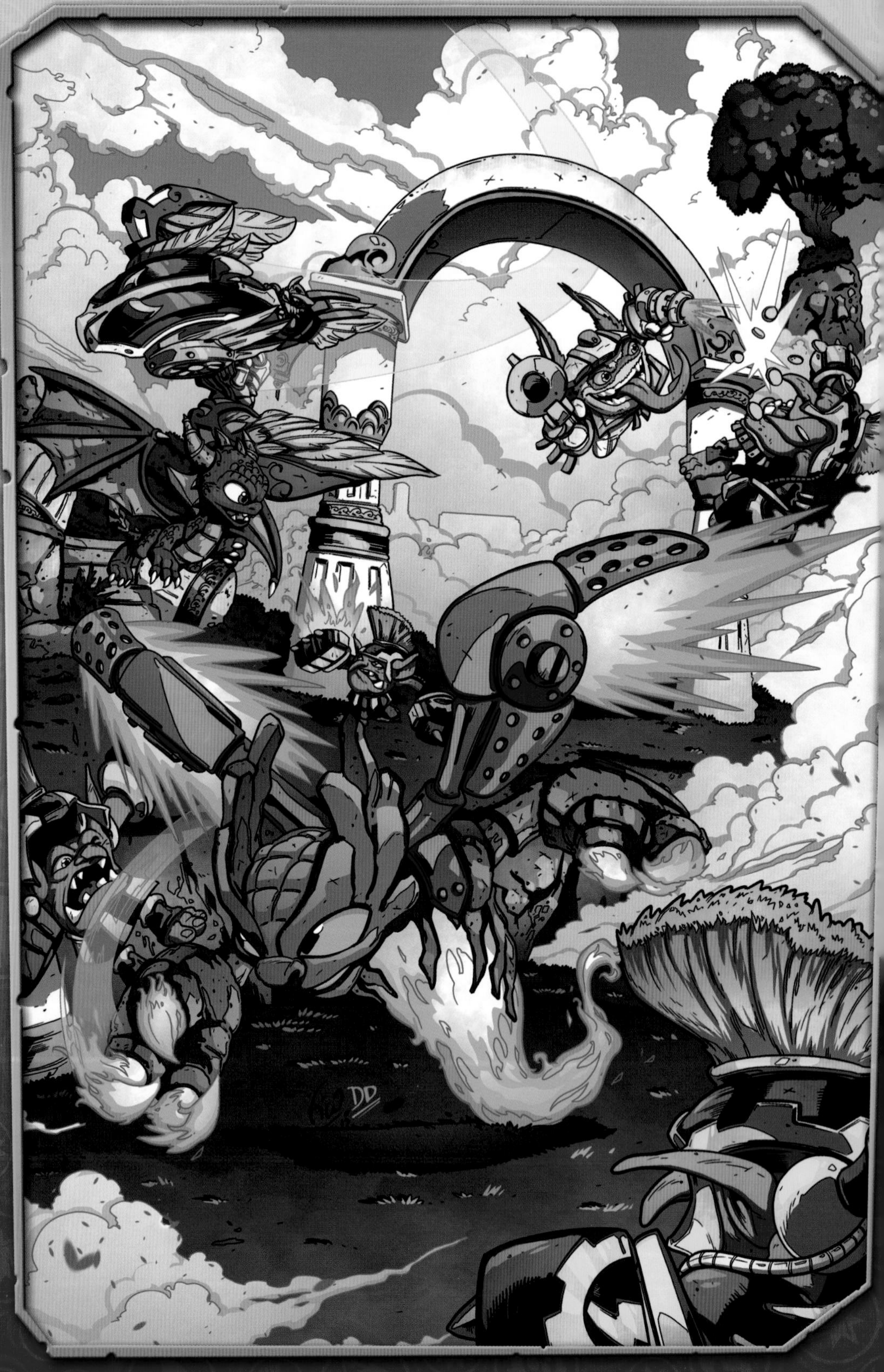

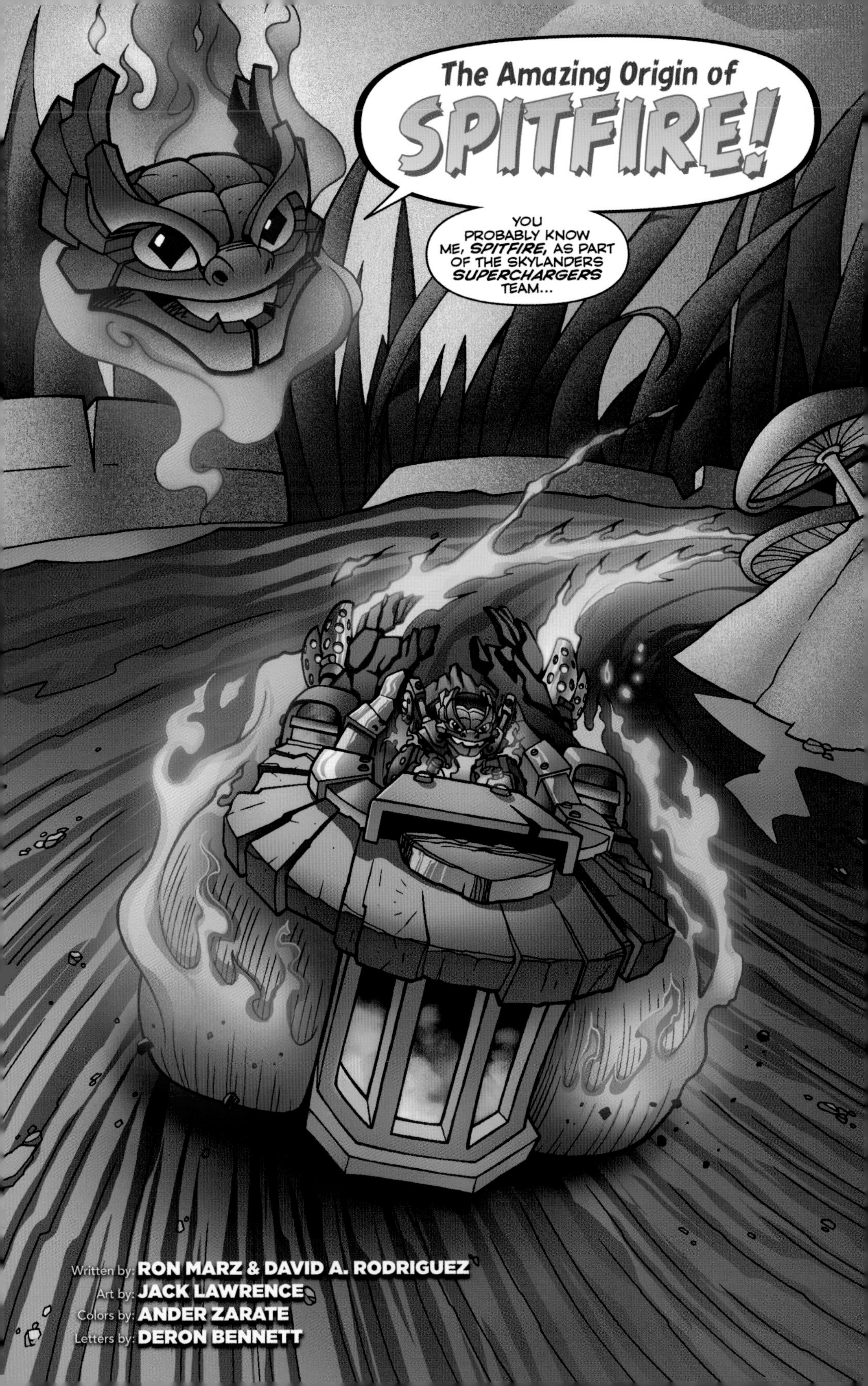

The Amazing Origin of SPITFIRE!
YOU PROBABLY KNOW ME, SPITFIRE, AS PART OF THE SKYLANDERS SUPERCHARGERS TEAM...
Written by: RON MARZ & DAVID A. RODRIGUEZ
Art by: JACK LAWRENCE
Colors by: ANDER ZARATE
Letters by: DERON BENNETT

"...BUT THAT'S NOT WHERE I GOT MY *START.*

"I WAS THE ONLY *FLAME SPIRIT* DRIVER IN THE SUPER SKYLAND'S RACING CIRCUIT, STEERING MY HOT STREAK AGAINST ANY AND ALL OPPONENTS.

"IF I DO SAY SO, WE MADE A PRETTY *UNBEATABLE* TEAM, AND WE WON ALMOST EVERY RACE ON THE CIRCUIT.

"THE FIRST RACE OF THAT SEASON'S CHAMPIONSHIP SERIES WOUND THROUGH *SIDEWINDER CANYON.*

"I WAS IN THE *LEAD,* ON MY WAY TO ANOTHER CHECKERED FLAG. BUT MY OPPONENTS HAD *OTHER* IDEAS.

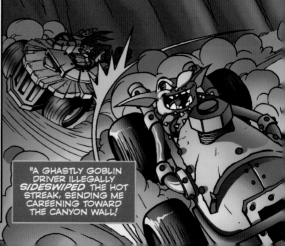

"A GHASTLY GOBLIN DRIVER ILLEGALLY *SIDESWIPED* THE HOT STREAK, SENDING ME CAREENING TOWARD THE CANYON WALL!

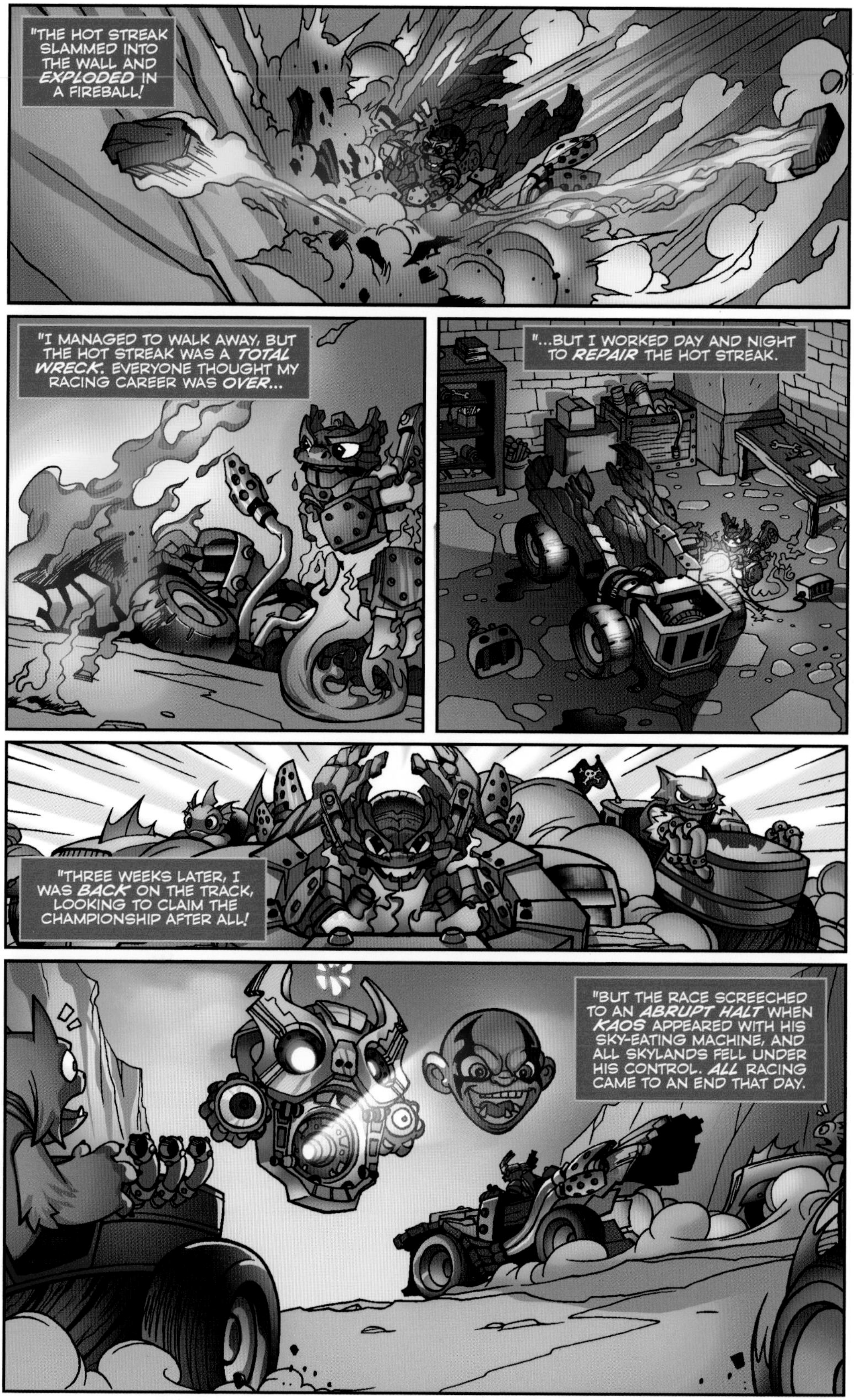
"THE HOT STREAK SLAMMED INTO THE WALL AND *EXPLODED* IN A FIREBALL!
"I MANAGED TO WALK AWAY, BUT THE HOT STREAK WAS A *TOTAL WRECK*. EVERYONE THOUGHT MY RACING CAREER WAS *OVER*...
"...BUT I WORKED DAY AND NIGHT TO *REPAIR* THE HOT STREAK.
"THREE WEEKS LATER, I WAS *BACK* ON THE TRACK, LOOKING TO CLAIM THE CHAMPIONSHIP AFTER ALL!
"BUT THE RACE SCREECHED TO AN *ABRUPT HALT* WHEN *KAOS* APPEARED WITH HIS SKY-EATING MACHINE, AND ALL SKYLANDS FELL UNDER HIS CONTROL. *ALL* RACING CAME TO AN END THAT DAY.

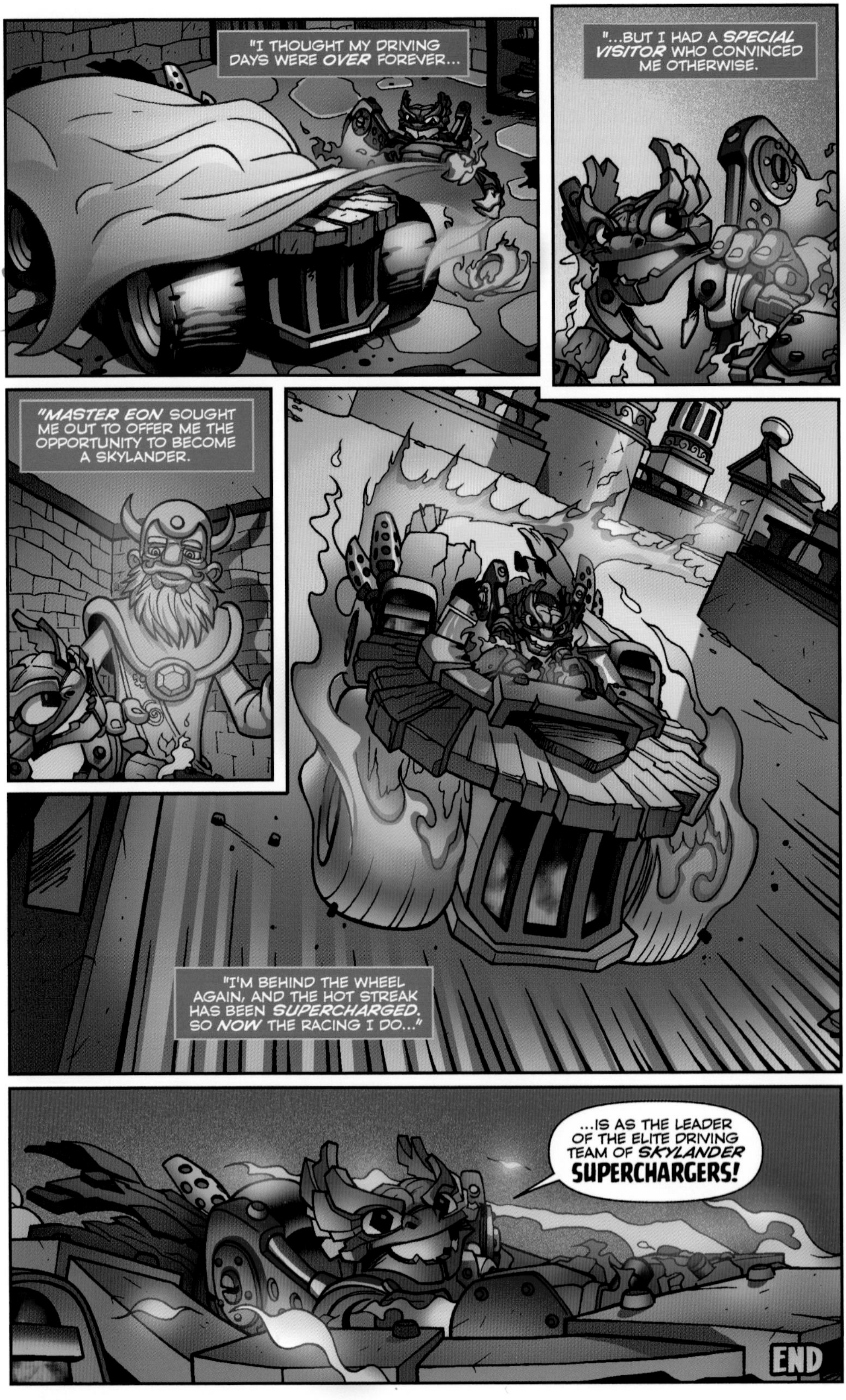
"I THOUGHT MY DRIVING DAYS WERE OVER FOREVER...
"...BUT I HAD A SPECIAL VISITOR WHO CONVINCED ME OTHERWISE.
"MASTER EON SOUGHT ME OUT TO OFFER ME THE OPPORTUNITY TO BECOME A SKYLANDER.
"I'M BEHIND THE WHEEL AGAIN, AND THE HOT STREAK HAS BEEN SUPERCHARGED. SO NOW THE RACING I DO..."
...IS AS THE LEADER OF THE ELITE DRIVING TEAM OF SKYLANDER SUPERCHARGERS!
END

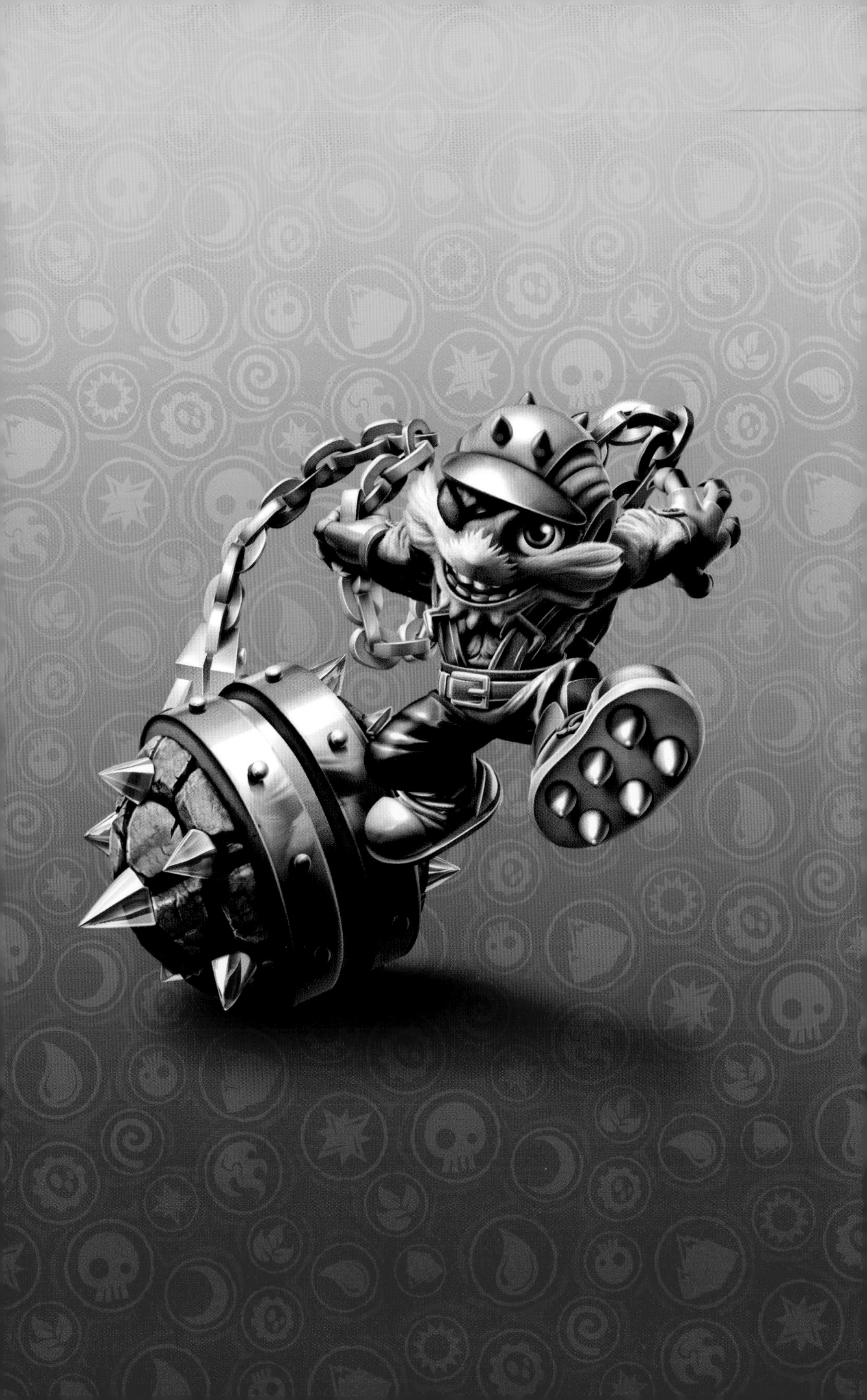

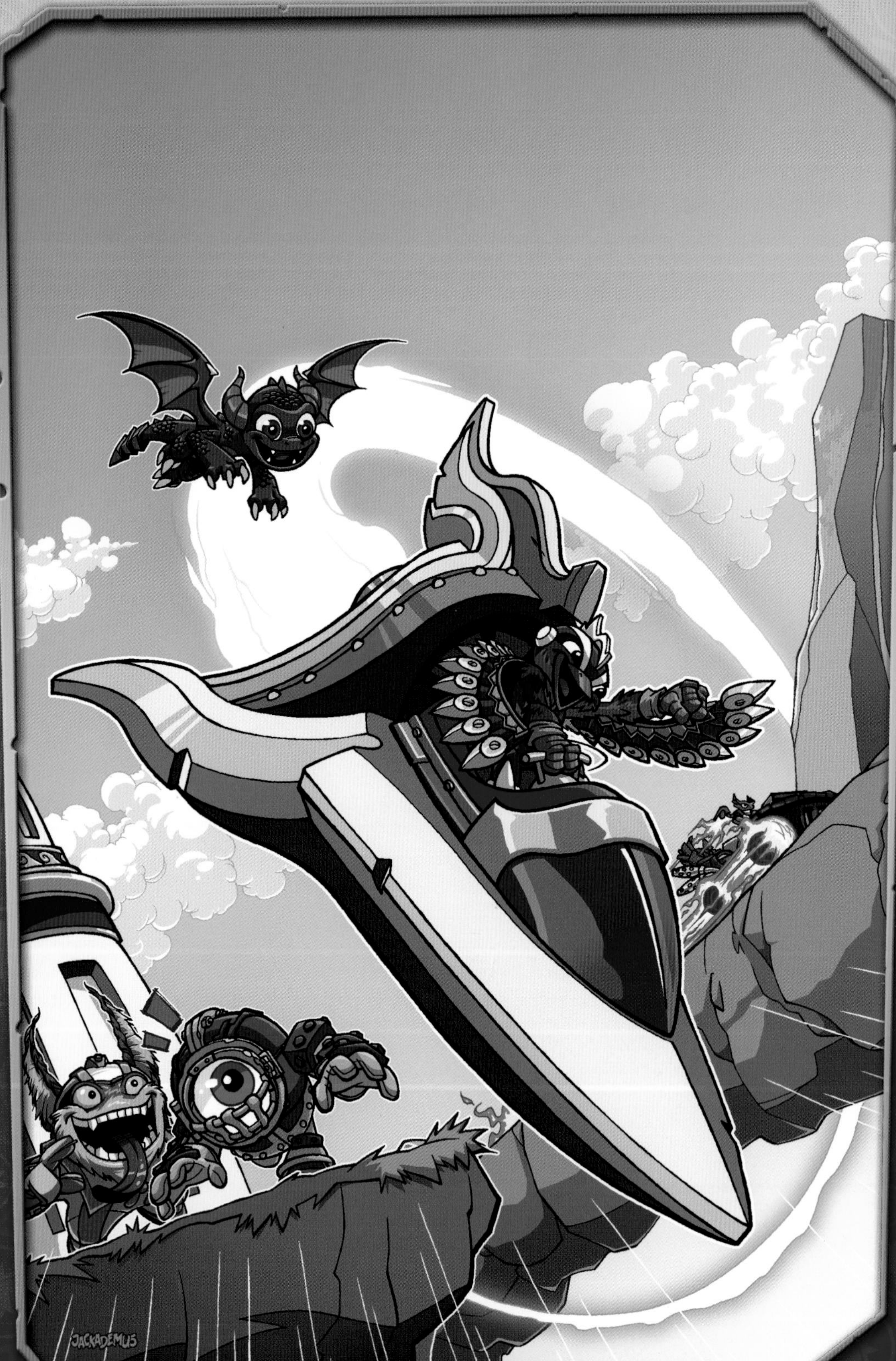
JACKADEMUS

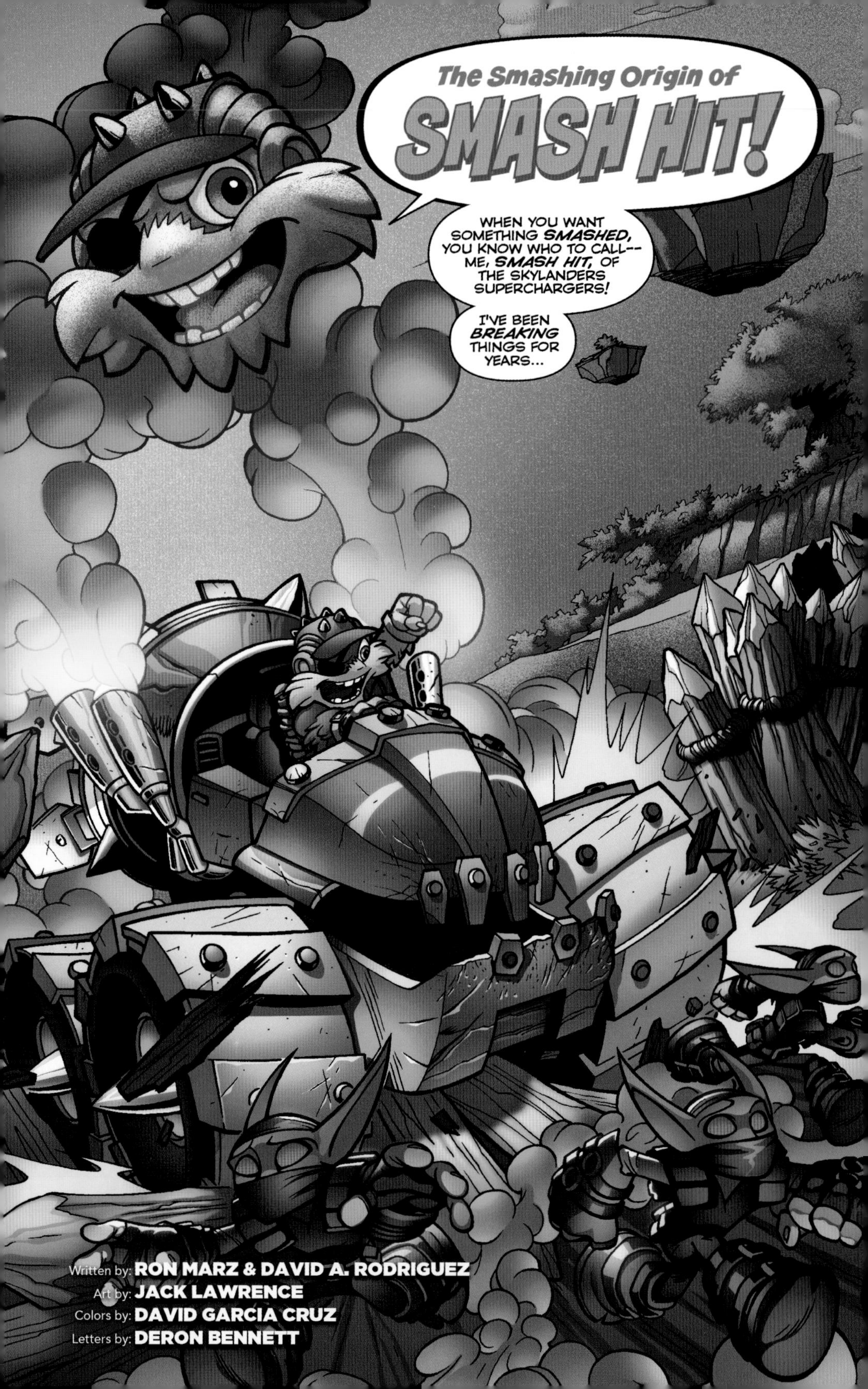
The Smashing Origin of
SMASH HIT!
WHEN YOU WANT SOMETHING SMASHED, YOU KNOW WHO TO CALL-- ME, SMASH HIT, OF THE SKYLANDERS SUPERCHARGERS!
I'VE BEEN BREAKING THINGS FOR YEARS...
Written by: RON MARZ & DAVID A. RODRIGUEZ
Art by: JACK LAWRENCE
Colors by: DAVID GARCIA CRUZ
Letters by: DERON BENNETT

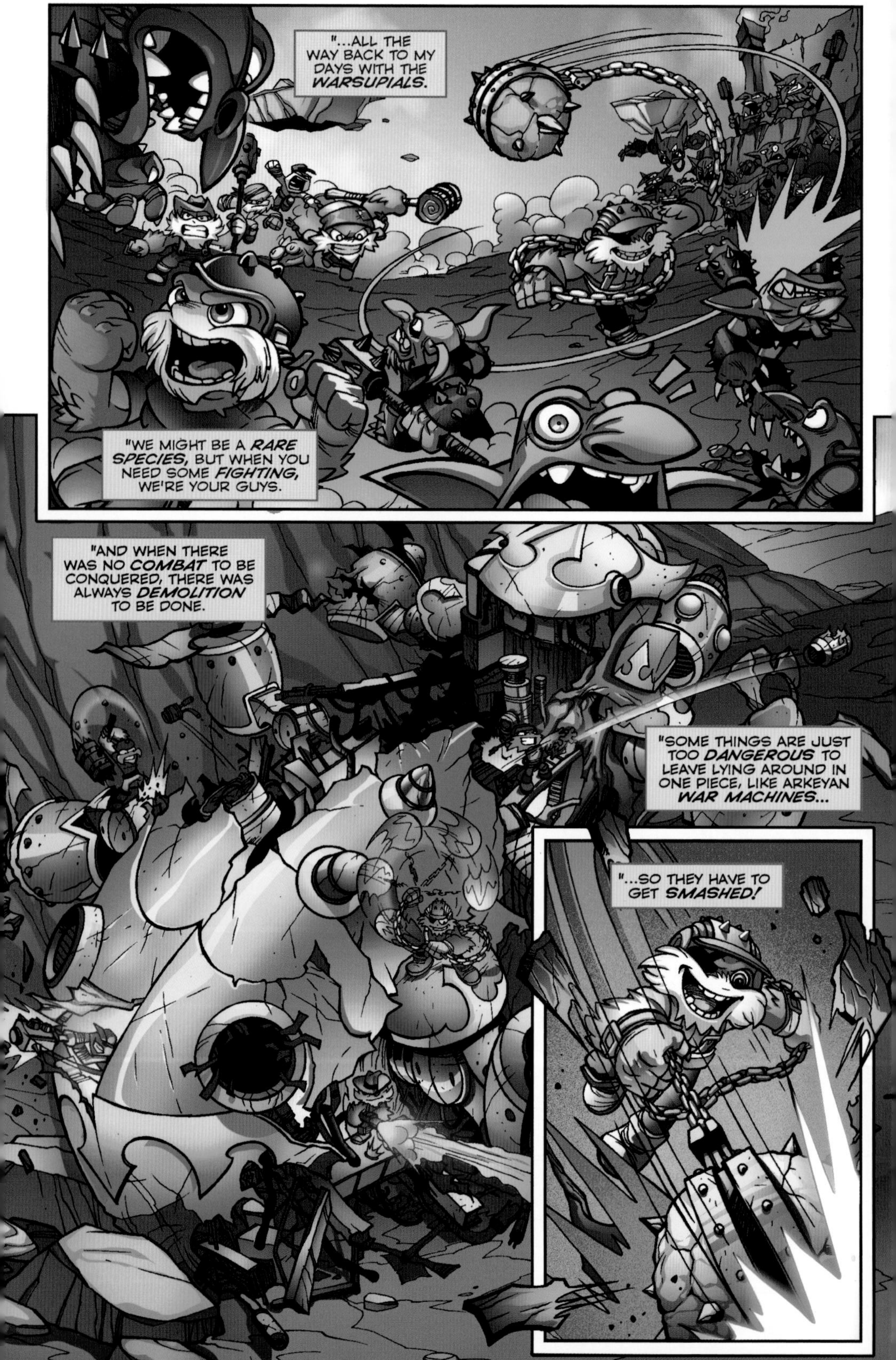
"...ALL THE WAY BACK TO MY DAYS WITH THE *WARSUPIALS*.
"WE MIGHT BE A *RARE SPECIES,* BUT WHEN YOU NEED SOME *FIGHTING,* WE'RE YOUR GUYS.
"AND WHEN THERE WAS NO *COMBAT* TO BE CONQUERED, THERE WAS ALWAYS *DEMOLITION* TO BE DONE.
"SOME THINGS ARE JUST TOO *DANGEROUS* TO LEAVE LYING AROUND IN ONE PIECE, LIKE ARKEYAN *WAR MACHINES*...
"...SO THEY HAVE TO GET *SMASHED!*

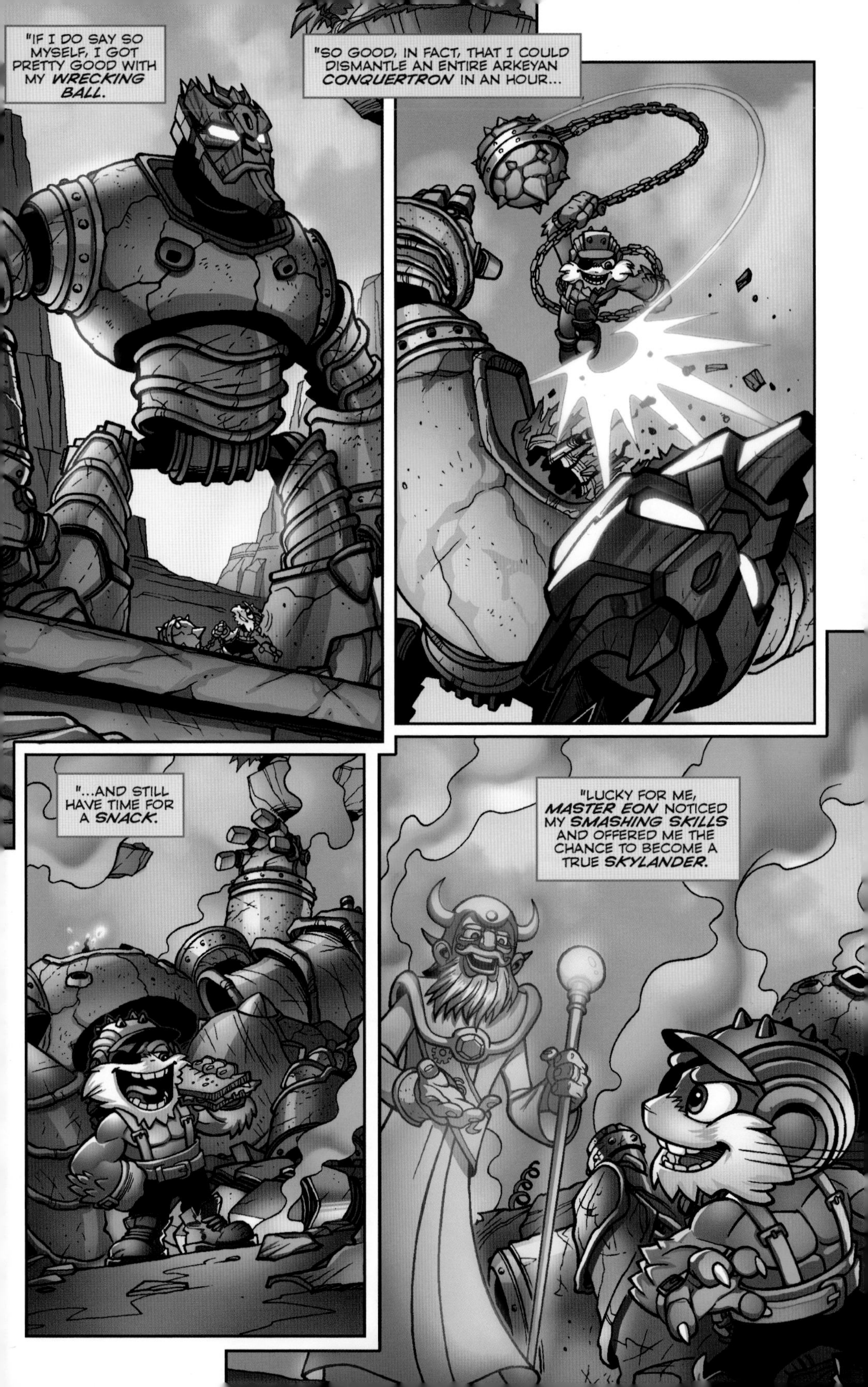
"IF I DO SAY SO MYSELF, I GOT PRETTY GOOD WITH MY WRECKING BALL.
"SO GOOD, IN FACT, THAT I COULD DISMANTLE AN ENTIRE ARKEYAN CONQUERTRON IN AN HOUR...
"...AND STILL HAVE TIME FOR A SNACK.
"LUCKY FOR ME, MASTER EON NOTICED MY SMASHING SKILLS AND OFFERED ME THE CHANCE TO BECOME A TRUE SKYLANDER.

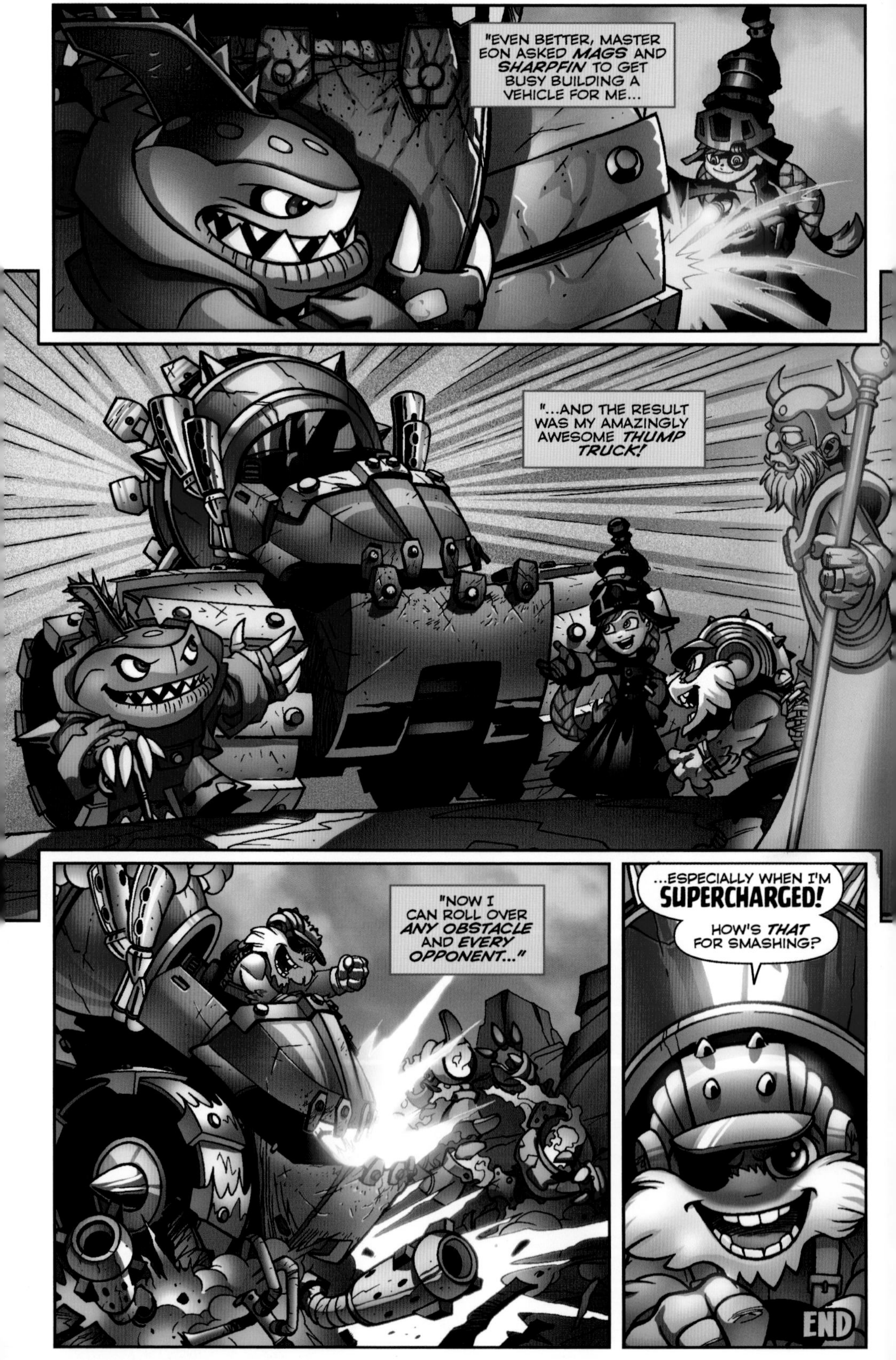
"EVEN BETTER, MASTER EON ASKED MAGS AND SHARPFIN TO GET BUSY BUILDING A VEHICLE FOR ME...
"...AND THE RESULT WAS MY AMAZINGLY AWESOME THUMP TRUCK!
"NOW I CAN ROLL OVER ANY OBSTACLE AND EVERY OPPONENT..."
...ESPECIALLY WHEN I'M SUPERCHARGED!
HOW'S THAT FOR SMASHING?
END

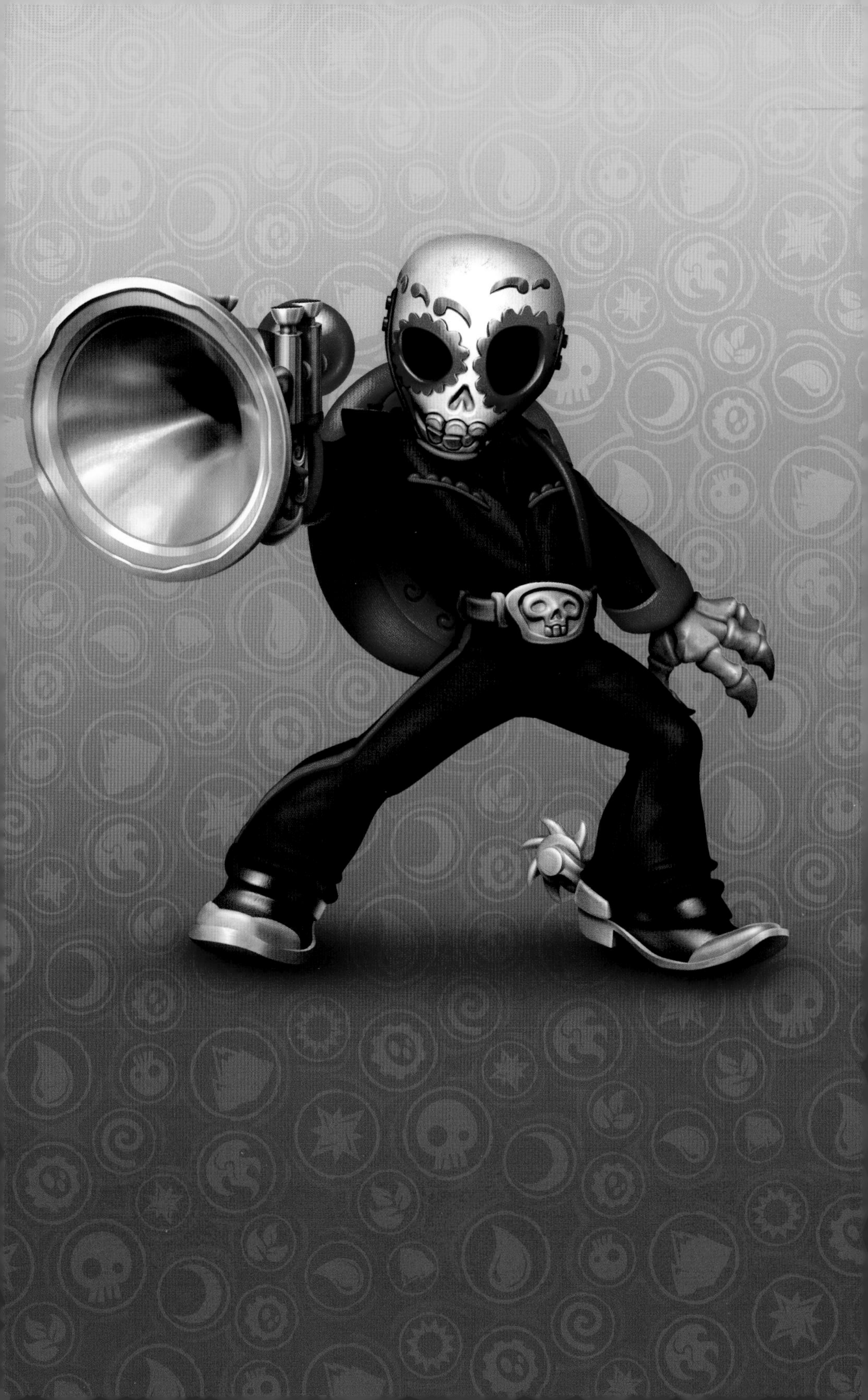

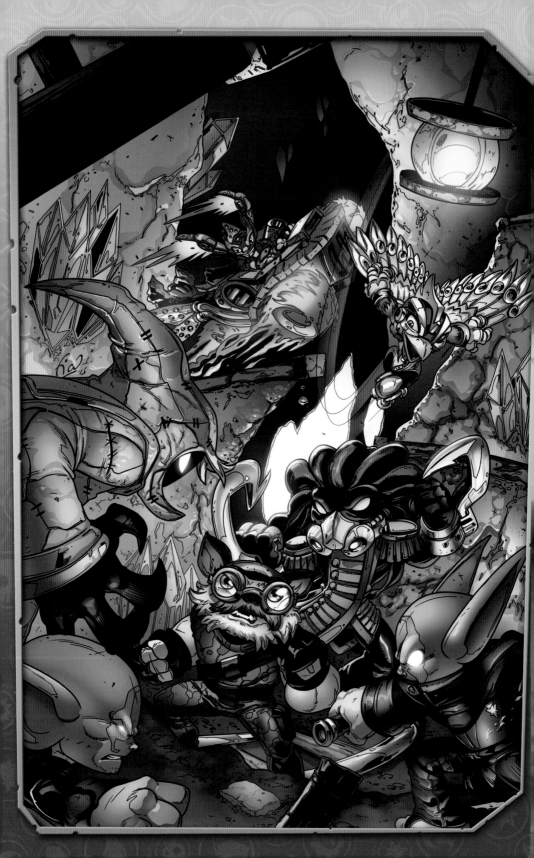

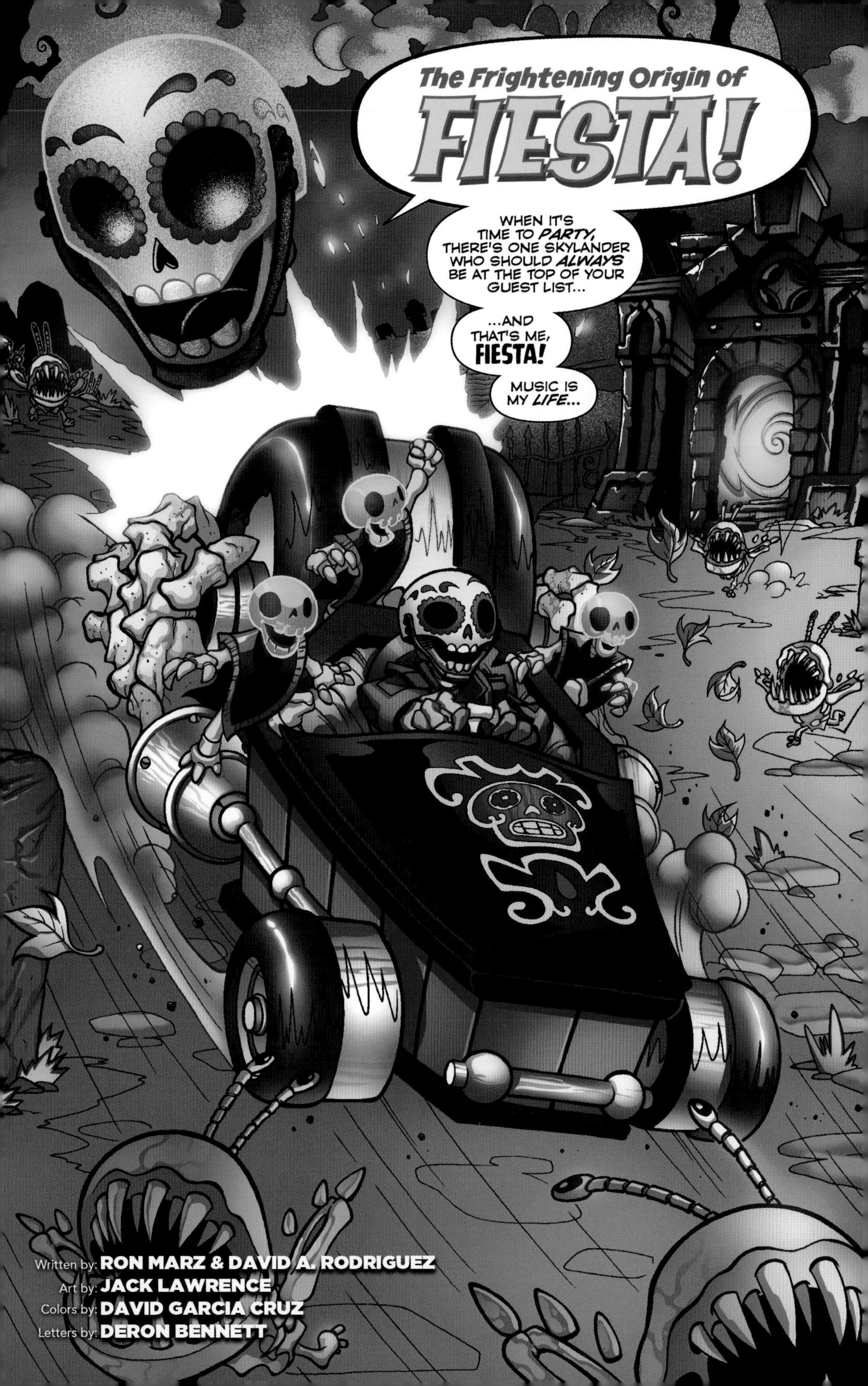
The Frightening Origin of
FIESTA!
WHEN IT'S TIME TO PARTY, THERE'S ONE SKYLANDER WHO SHOULD ALWAYS BE AT THE TOP OF YOUR GUEST LIST...
...AND THAT'S ME, FIESTA!
MUSIC IS MY LIFE...
Written by: RON MARZ & DAVID A. RODRIGUEZ
Art by: JACK LAWRENCE
Colors by: DAVID GARCIA CRUZ
Letters by: DERON BENNETT

"...ESPECIALLY MY TRUSTY *TRUMPET.*

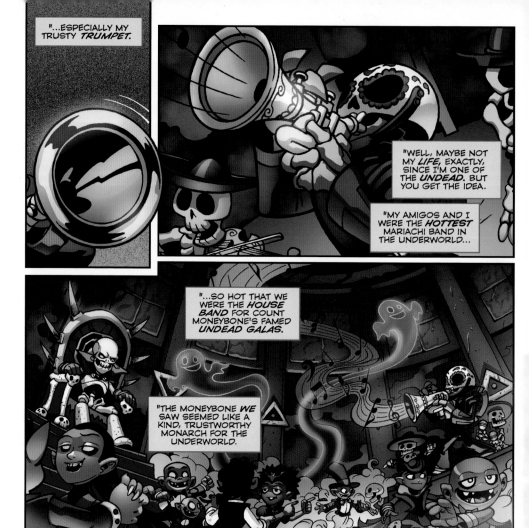

"WELL, MAYBE NOT MY *LIFE,* EXACTLY, SINCE I'M ONE OF THE *UNDEAD.* BUT YOU GET THE IDEA.

"MY AMIGOS AND I WERE THE *HOTTEST* MARIACHI BAND IN THE UNDERWORLD...

"...SO HOT THAT WE WERE THE *HOUSE BAND* FOR COUNT MONEYBONE'S FAMED *UNDEAD GALAS.*

"THE MONEYBONE *WE* SAW SEEMED LIKE A KIND, TRUSTWORTHY MONARCH FOR THE UNDERWORLD.

"WE EVEN TOOK IT UPON OURSELVES TO *WELCOME* NEW ARRIVALS TO THE UNDERWORLD WITH OUR MUSIC.

"THEN ONE DAY A VERY *PARTICULAR* GROUP OF NEW ARRIVALS APPEARED. I WAS THE ONLY ONE WHO REALIZED THEY WERE ACTUALLY *SKYLANDERS* IN DISGUISE...

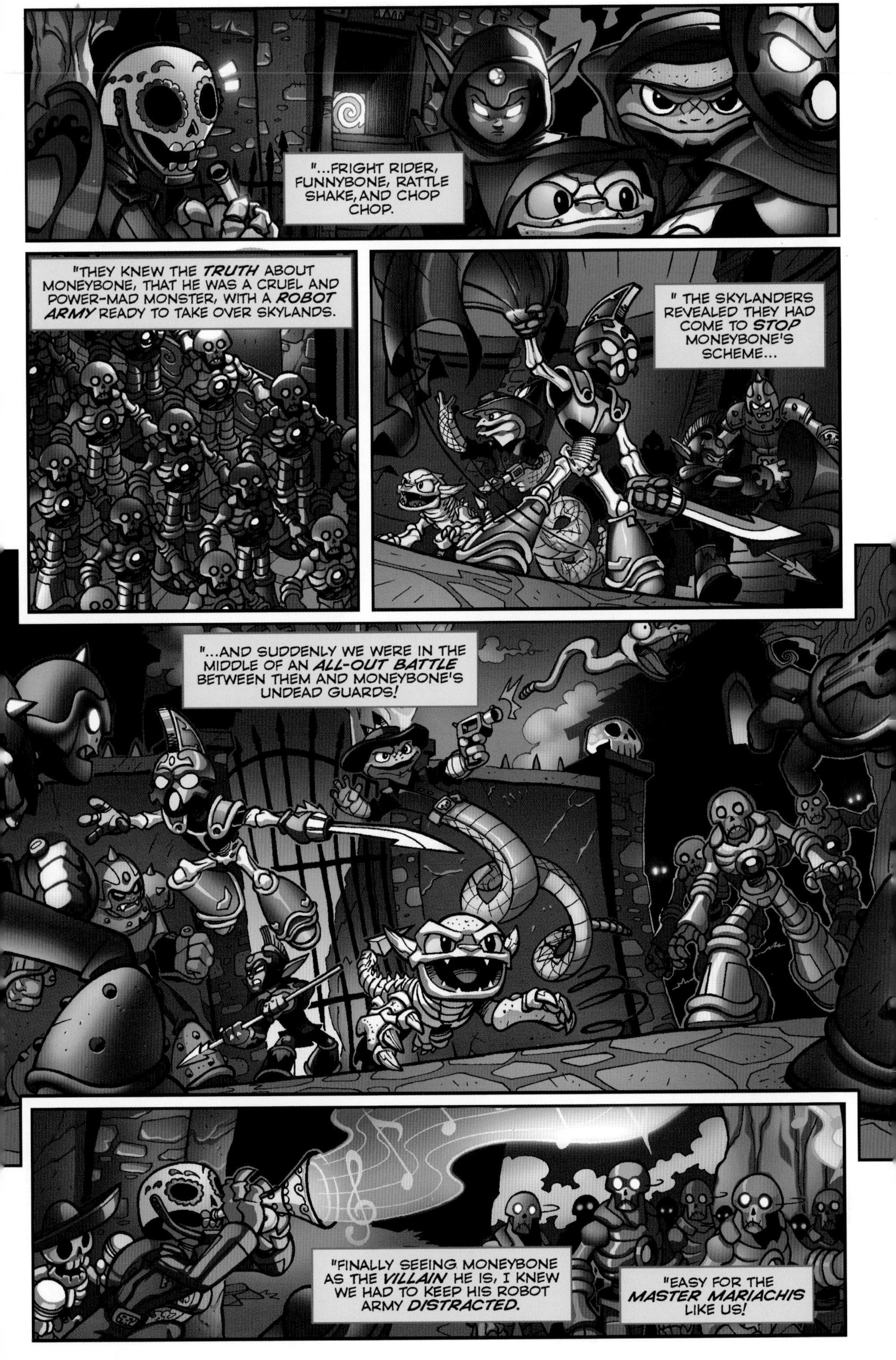
"...FRIGHT RIDER, FUNNYBONE, RATTLE SHAKE, AND CHOP CHOP.
"THEY KNEW THE TRUTH ABOUT MONEYBONE, THAT HE WAS A CRUEL AND POWER-MAD MONSTER, WITH A ROBOT ARMY READY TO TAKE OVER SKYLANDS.
" THE SKYLANDERS REVEALED THEY HAD COME TO STOP MONEYBONE'S SCHEME...
"...AND SUDDENLY WE WERE IN THE MIDDLE OF AN ALL-OUT BATTLE BETWEEN THEM AND MONEYBONE'S UNDEAD GUARDS!
"FINALLY SEEING MONEYBONE AS THE VILLAIN HE IS, I KNEW WE HAD TO KEEP HIS ROBOT ARMY DISTRACTED.
"EASY FOR THE MASTER MARIACHIS LIKE US!

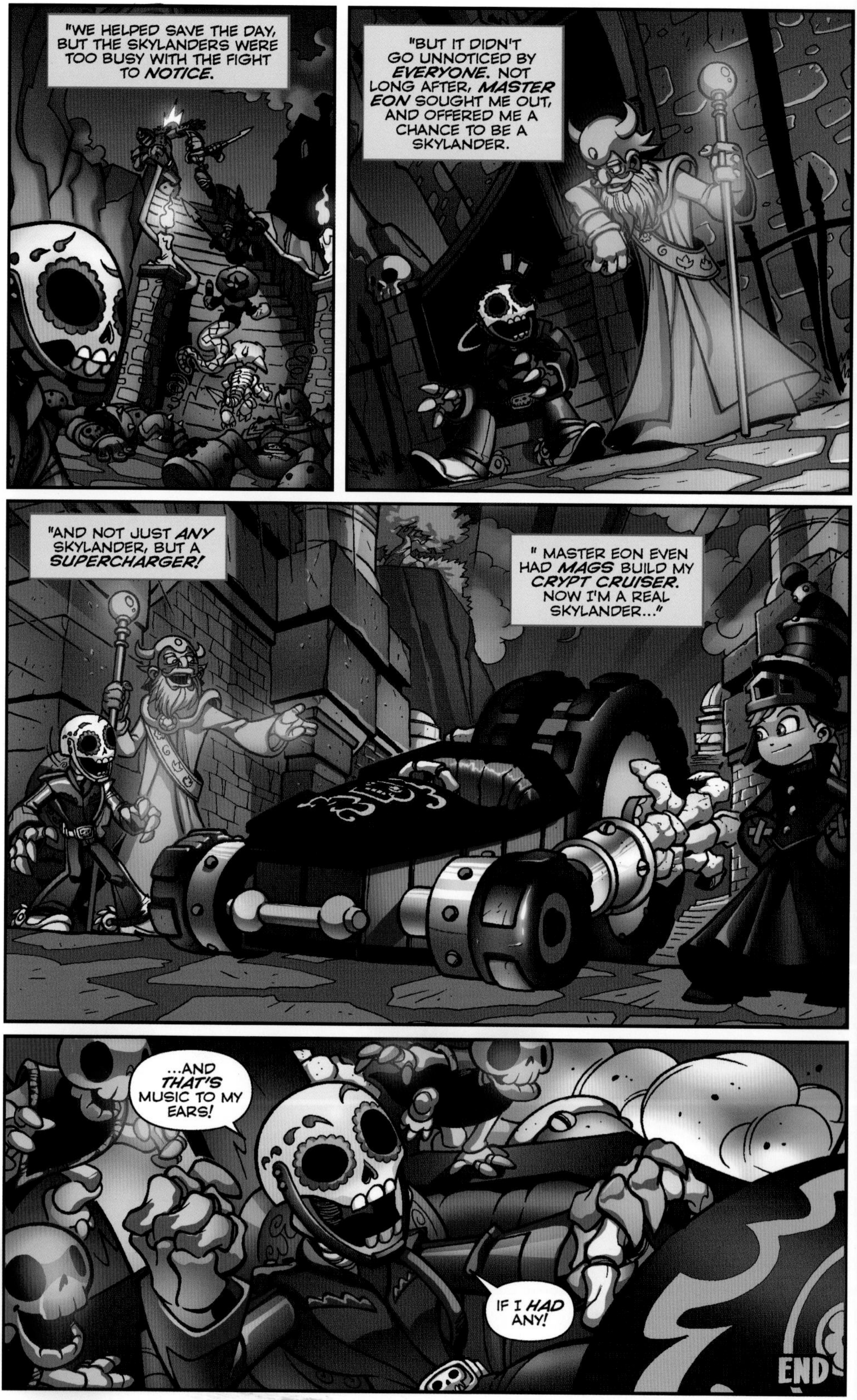
"WE HELPED SAVE THE DAY, BUT THE SKYLANDERS WERE TOO BUSY WITH THE FIGHT TO *NOTICE*.
"BUT IT DIDN'T GO UNNOTICED BY *EVERYONE*. NOT LONG AFTER, *MASTER EON* SOUGHT ME OUT, AND OFFERED ME A CHANCE TO BE A SKYLANDER.
"AND NOT JUST *ANY* SKYLANDER, BUT A *SUPERCHARGER!*
" MASTER EON EVEN HAD *MAGS* BUILD MY *CRYPT CRUISER*. NOW I'M A REAL SKYLANDER..."
...AND *THAT'S* MUSIC TO MY EARS!
IF I *HAD* ANY!
END

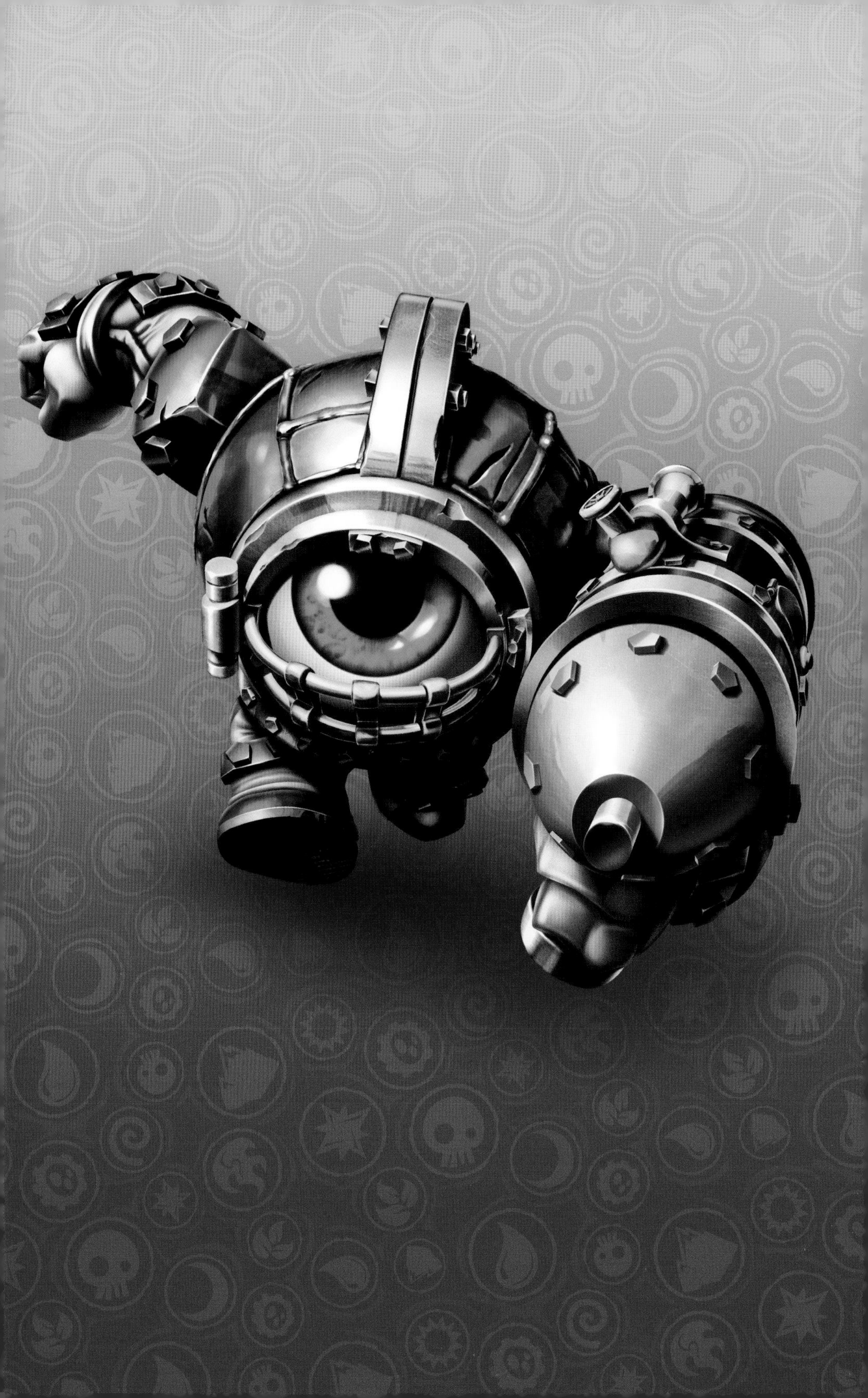

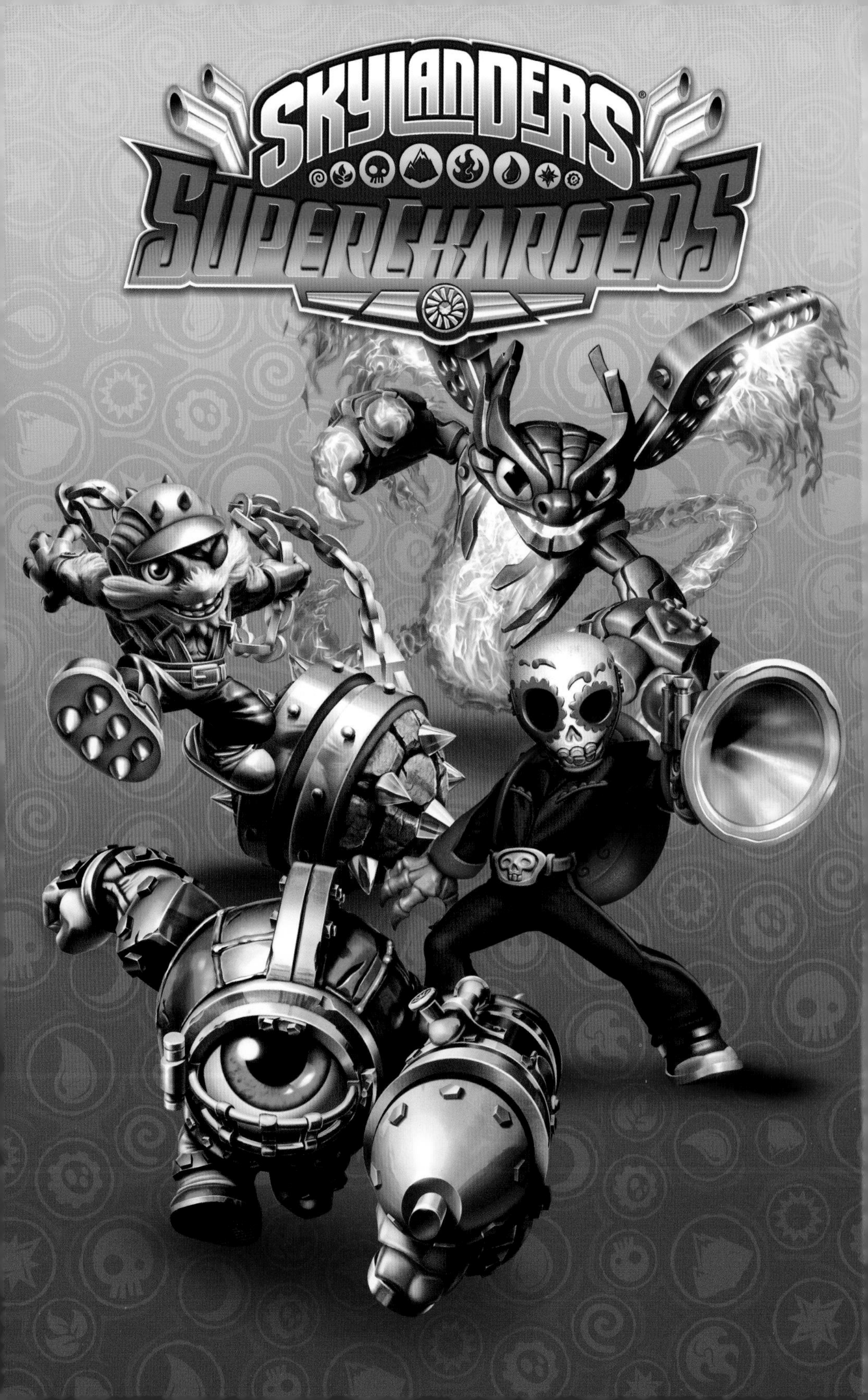
SKYLANDERS
SUPERCHARGERS

DIVE-CLOPS

BIO

Believe it or not, *Dive-Clops* is actually the twin brother of Eye-Brawl. When he was young, his batwings were blasted off by pirates while he was flying over the Swirling Sea, causing him to plunge into the abyss below. After rolling on the bottom for several days, he was discovered by an underwater civilization of Jelly Dwarves. They were instantly fascinated by the bizarre looking eyeball and took him back to their Coral Castle, where they built him a magnificent dive suit that would allow him to explore the depths of the sea. But everything changed when *Dive-Clops* decided to venture to the mysterious Whirlpool of Destiny deep within the ocean. As he got closer, he suddenly felt pulled by its immense power, and reemerged to discover that thousands of years had passed! Now with his destiny before him as a member of the Skylanders, *Dive-Clops* lets the minions of Kaos know that there are many dangers of the deep!

FIESTA

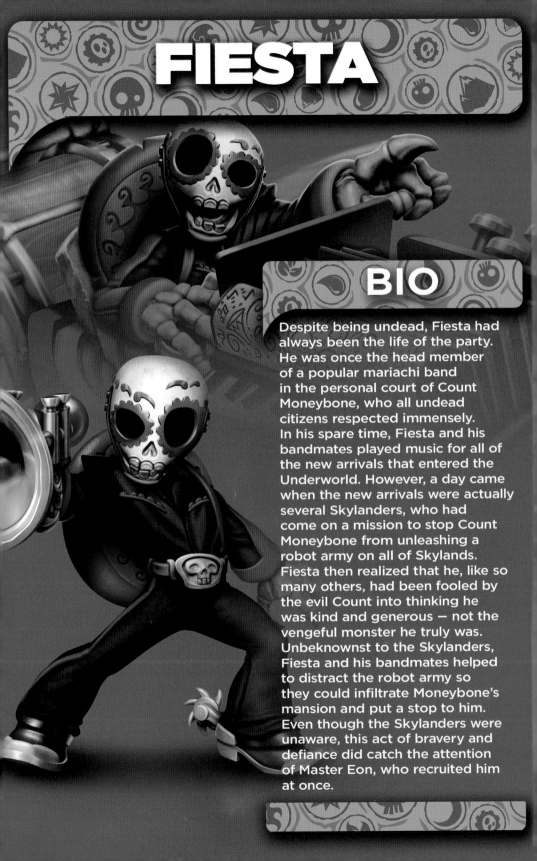

BIO

Despite being undead, Fiesta had always been the life of the party. He was once the head member of a popular mariachi band in the personal court of Count Moneybone, who all undead citizens respected immensely. In his spare time, Fiesta and his bandmates played music for all of the new arrivals that entered the Underworld. However, a day came when the new arrivals were actually several Skylanders, who had come on a mission to stop Count Moneybone from unleashing a robot army on all of Skylands. Fiesta then realized that he, like so many others, had been fooled by the evil Count into thinking he was kind and generous — not the vengeful monster he truly was. Unbeknownst to the Skylanders, Fiesta and his bandmates helped to distract the robot army so they could infiltrate Moneybone's mansion and put a stop to him. Even though the Skylanders were unaware, this act of bravery and defiance did catch the attention of Master Eon, who recruited him at once.

SMASH HIT

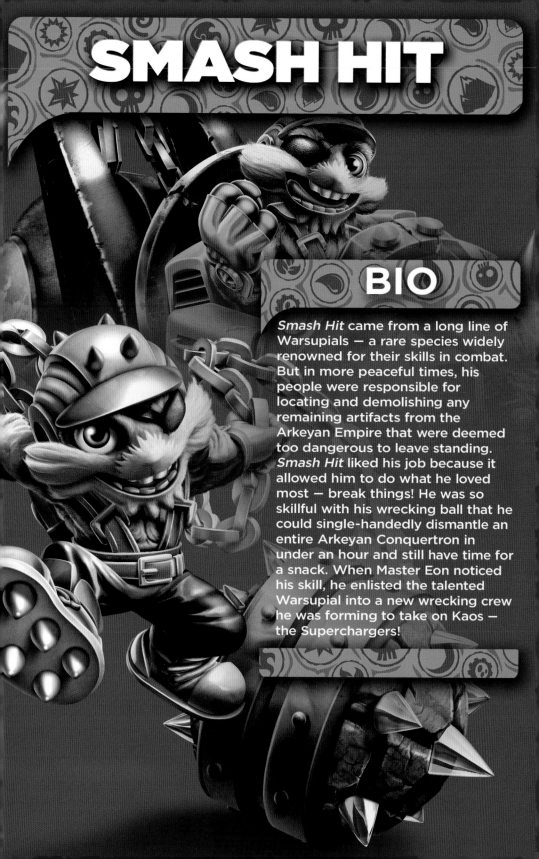

BIO

Smash Hit came from a long line of Warsupials — a rare species widely renowned for their skills in combat. But in more peaceful times, his people were responsible for locating and demolishing any remaining artifacts from the Arkeyan Empire that were deemed too dangerous to leave standing. *Smash Hit* liked his job because it allowed him to do what he loved most — break things! He was so skillful with his wrecking ball that he could single-handedly dismantle an entire Arkeyan Conquertron in under an hour and still have time for a snack. When Master Eon noticed his skill, he enlisted the talented Warsupial into a new wrecking crew he was forming to take on Kaos — the Superchargers!

SPITFIRE

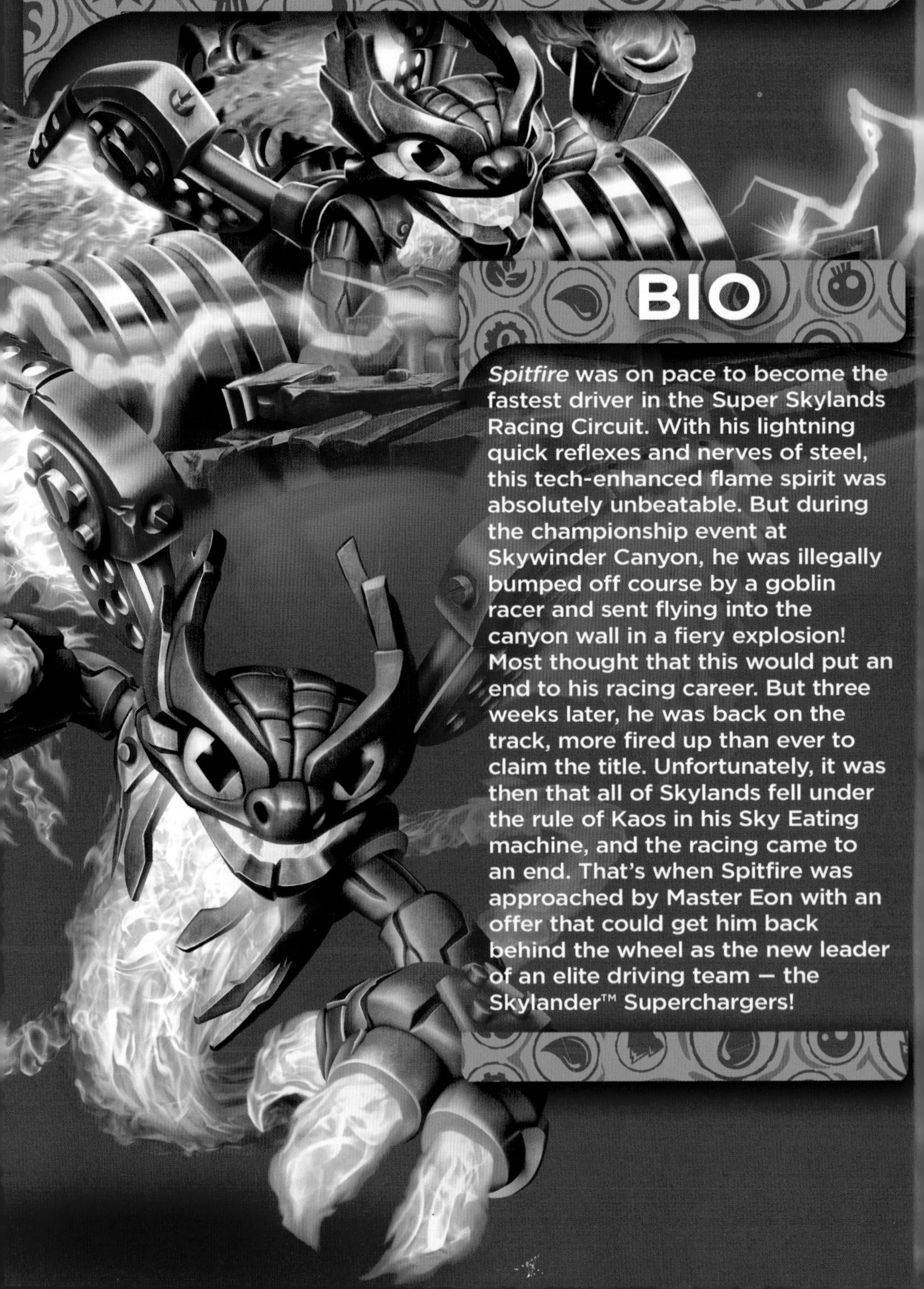

BIO

Spitfire was on pace to become the fastest driver in the Super Skylands Racing Circuit. With his lightning quick reflexes and nerves of steel, this tech-enhanced flame spirit was absolutely unbeatable. But during the championship event at Skywinder Canyon, he was illegally bumped off course by a goblin racer and sent flying into the canyon wall in a fiery explosion! Most thought that this would put an end to his racing career. But three weeks later, he was back on the track, more fired up than ever to claim the title. Unfortunately, it was then that all of Skylands fell under the rule of Kaos in his Sky Eating machine, and the racing came to an end. That's when Spitfire was approached by Master Eon with an offer that could get him back behind the wheel as the new leader of an elite driving team — the Skylander™ Superchargers!

Art by: **JACK LAWRANCE**

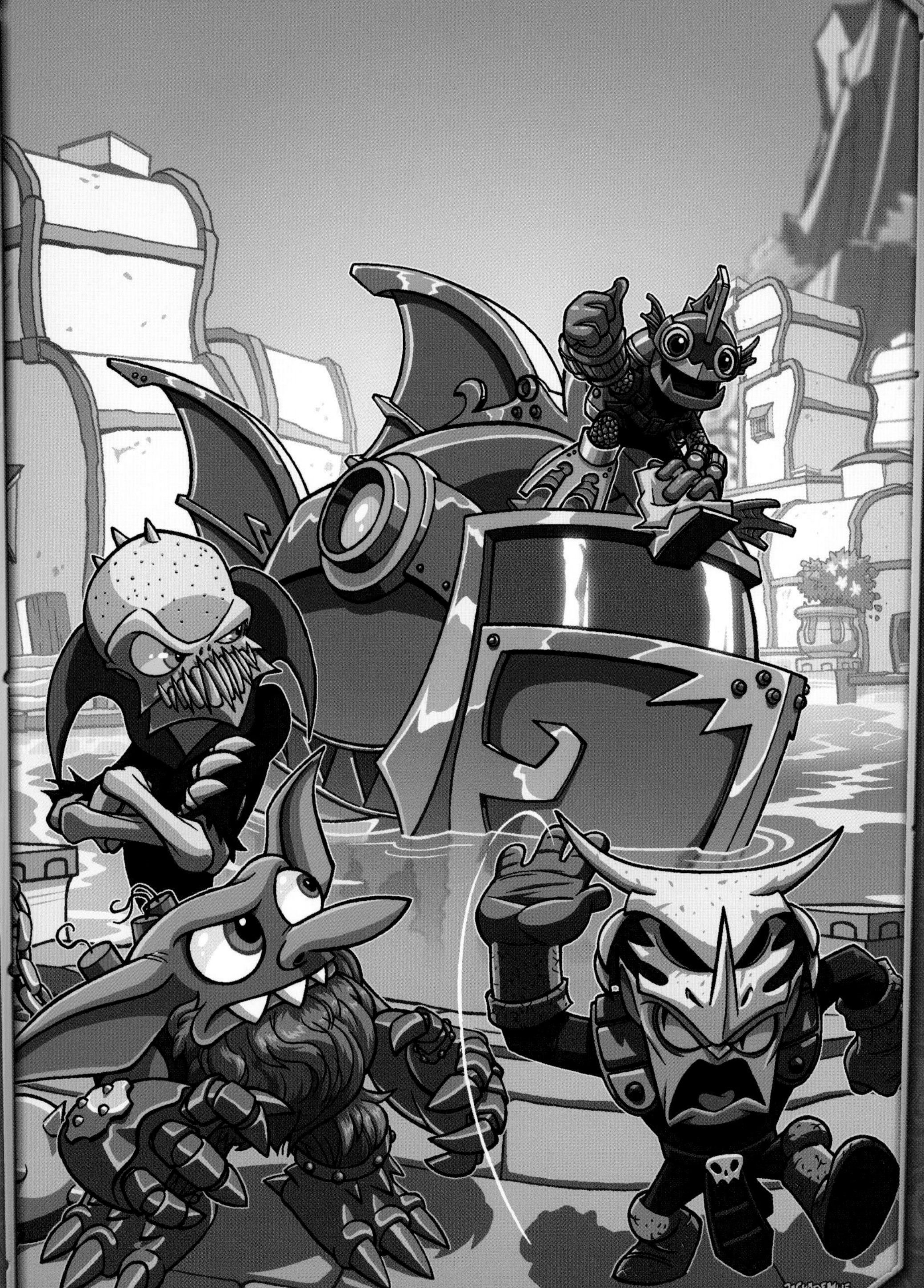

JACKADEMUS

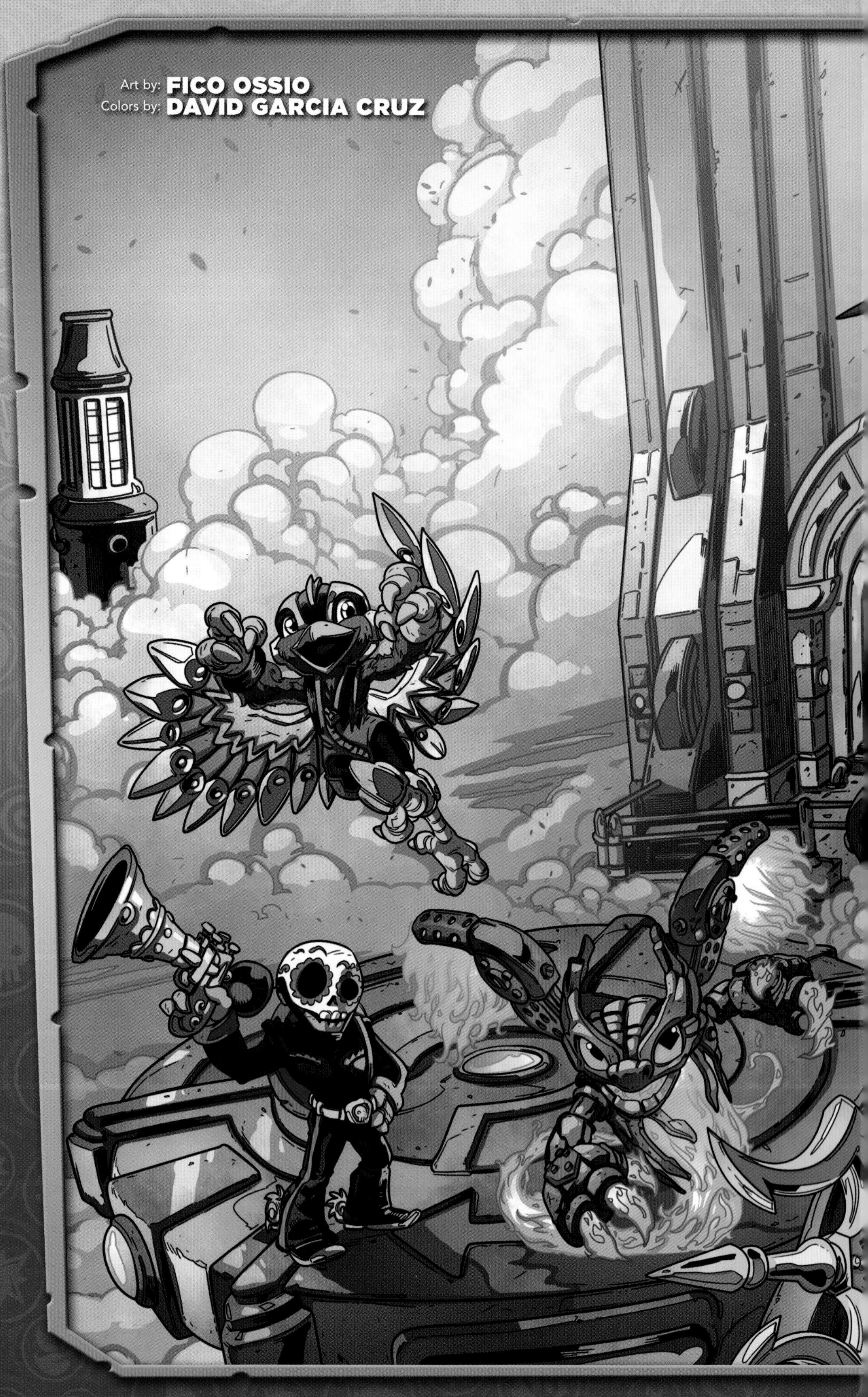
Art by: FICO OSSIO
Colors by: DAVID GARCIA CRUZ

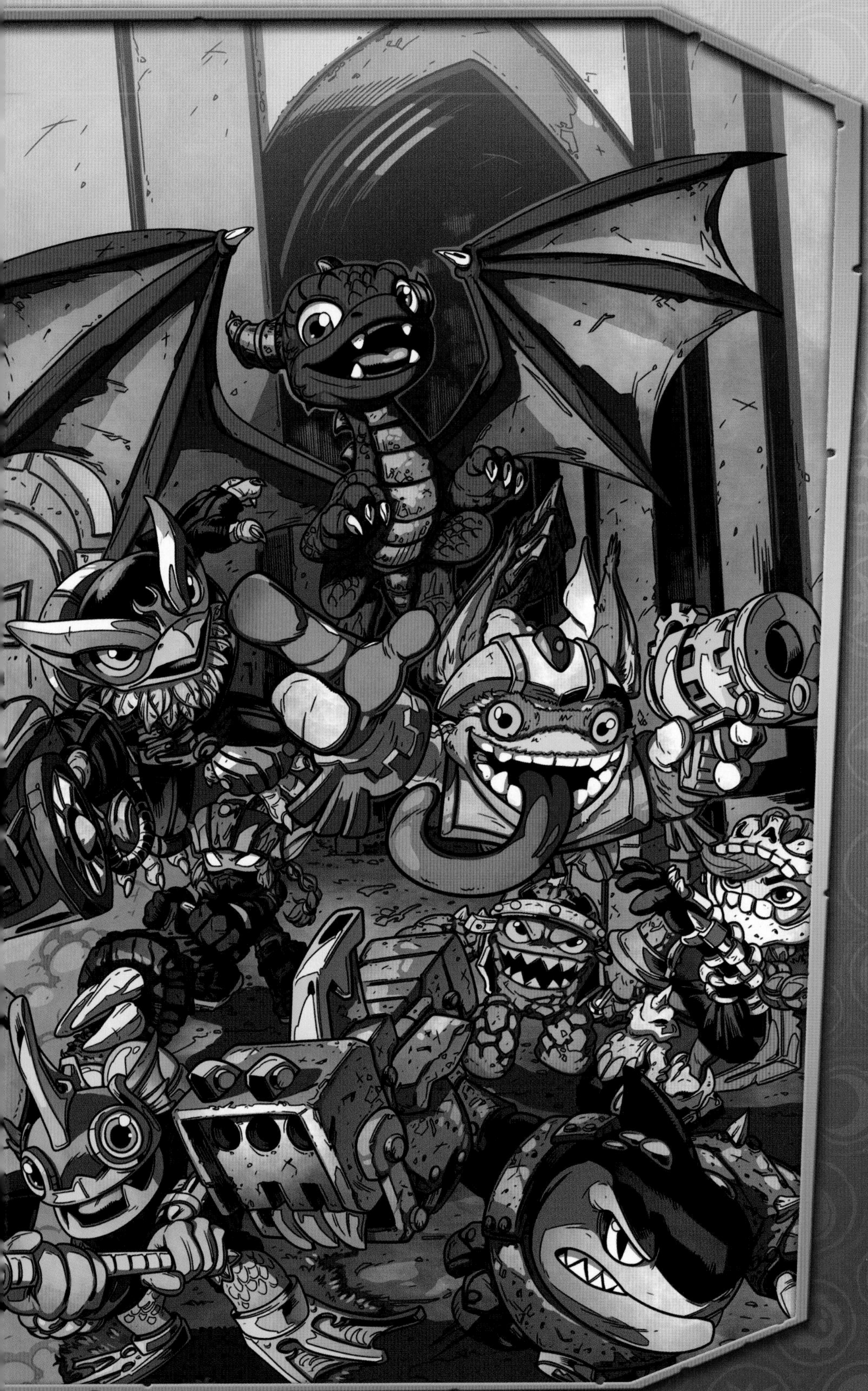